'Aren't you capable of making a judgement yourself, Miss Maynard? I was expecting a great deal more from a nurse trained at St Mary's and then at Oswestry. I'm a Thomas man myself.'

Bright colour rose in Alison's face until it felt as if her cheeks were glowing like red hot coals. A Thomas man indeed! You could always tell a Thomas man, but you could never tell a Thomas man anything.

'I've done my level best in the time, Dr Zeke. I don't think you quite understand——'

'I understand that you, like any new member of staff, are under three months' trial as a probationer. My patients must get the best possible treatment, and I shan't think twice about dismissing you if you don't come up to standard.'

Sara Burton was convent educated and trained as a physiotherapist at a school in the Midlands. She has worked in England, Scandinavia and North America and received her B.Sc. in Physical Therapy from a Western Canadian University. Currently she is engaged in independent research related to partial dislocations of joints in the lower limb. She is a bird fancier with special interest in homing pigeons.

Previous Titles

HEART SEARCHING
EXPERT TREATMENT
DR ROSKILDE'S RETURN
A MEDICAL OPINION

HAWAIIAN HEALING

BY

SARA BURTON

MILLS & BOON LIMITED
ETON HOUSE 18–24 PARADISE ROAD
RICHMOND SURREY TW9 1SR

First published in Great Britain 1991
by Mills & Boon Limited

This edition 1991

ISBN 0 263 77318 3

Set in 11½ on 13 pt Linotron Palatino
03-9107-38564
Typeset in Great Britain by Centracet, Cambridge
Made and printed in Great Britain

CHAPTER ONE

'KEEP it down to a low roar, please, boys!' Charge Nurse Alison Maynard quipped easily.

Orthopaedic Ward 419 here in this Hawaiian hospital was just like any other in the world. The men in this four-bedder room were all on traction for fractured femurs, so they weren't ill, just generally bored most of the time.

'It's a fashion parade!' and, 'I like the new nurse's uniform!' had been the goodnatured yells as Alison had entered their room. Now they clapped and cheered at her answer. And she couldn't help laughing back.

Their reaction didn't surprise her, because she had been asked to start her new job unexpectedly early, and because she hadn't yet been issued with the usual white uniform she was dressed in her British one of navy and white and black stockings.

She had been about to be introduced to each patient on the ward, but her senior, Mary Amos, had been called away to the telephone.

Now she introduced herself and chatted to each patient in turn.

Mary was engaged for so long that Alison decided to continue her tour alone. She would be in charge of the ward this evening, and if she knew the patients and they knew her it was less likely that anything desperate would happen.

But as Alison was about to enter another room Mary strode up. She was older, in her middle forties, and it was clear that the ward was run on precision.

'I heard the men shouting their approval, Alison. I don't think they'll have any complaints tonight.'

'I think it's the uniform,' Alison admitted.

Mary chuckled goodnaturedly. 'Then they'd better make the most of it, because come Monday you'll be in standard issue pure white.' She consulted her fob watch. 'I think I'll introduce you to Ross Kelso first.'

In the single room Alison stared down at the unconscious boy in his hospital bed. So it was true: you couldn't run away from your problems. And at that moment she knew she was about to come face to face with her painful past.

Mary stood on the opposite side of the bed and stroked the boy's hair. Like all good nurses, she spoke to her patient as if he could understand, because it was surprising what patients would remember once they came round.

'Listen, Ross, we've got a new nurse on the ward. And she's come all the way from England to treat you here. What do you think of that?'

Alison slipped her hand into the boy's and squeezed hard. 'Hello, Ross,' she said, a little too softly. Then more loudly, 'I'm sure a lot of the techniques we use in England will be very helpful to you and that you'll soon be fully recovered.'

She squeezed his hand again, but there was no response. His eyes were open but staring; they did not comprehend.

She felt a lump grow in her throat. He was reminding her of her fiancé. Thank God he had died quickly after his head injury in a motorbike accident.

After a little more talk, Mary signalled to Alison to put up the cot sides. 'We'll have to leave you now, Ross. I have to introduce Miss Maynard to all the other patients on the ward. She'll come back later on and talk to you again.'

Once in the corridor and out of earshot Mary became sombre. 'Ross is a particularly sad case. The result of drunk driving, and, worse still, a hit-and-run accident.'

Alison felt her breath catch in her throat.

Mary continued, 'Yes, if it hadn't been for a courting couple on that dark road, the drunk driver, Bill Noxley, would have got away with it. They noted down his car number and went to help Ross immediately.'

Alison's legs began to tremble. 'I thought you didn't have head injuries on this particular orthopaedic ward?' This was the very reason she had chosen Ward 419.

'We have two orthopaedic surgeons on this ward,' Mary explained. 'Old Dr Armstrong, who's about to retire, and isn't around much, and his son. The younger doctor is known as Dr Zeke to avoid confusion. Now, Ross belongs to Dr Zeke, and he decided that the boy might do better on this side of the hospital because the noise of the traffic might startle him back to life. It's unusual, but he's the only head injury I expect you'll see on this ward.'

It became clear to Alison that she would have to try and put aside her emotional feelings, but she wasn't sure if she could be totally detached and uninvolved.

Seeing Alison's troubled expression, Mary said, 'Don't worry about the doctors. I don't expect you'll see old Dr Armstrong tonight.

And Dr Zeke is away in New York for a conference. He won't be back until later next week.'

Alison tried to look a little more relaxed; she didn't want Mary to know that she had been thinking of her fiancé's death.

Mary smiled. 'You know, I really can't thank you enough for coming in at such short notice to look after the ward. After all, you shouldn't start work until Monday. But I'm so grateful, because I must have a talk with my daughter's teachers. She's having real problems with her maths.'

'It's no trouble at all.' Alison sounded confident now. 'In fact, I welcome the chance to get to know the patients before the usual hurly-burly of the ward day.'

She was introduced to the rest of the patients and made to feel very welcome. She decided that she'd enjoy working here.

The unit was typical of orthopaedics. It consisted of two- and four-bedded rooms. The men were all young and traumatic injuries, and the women were mostly joint replacements and fractures.

When Mary was satisfied that she had explained everything she again thanked Alison. 'I don't think you'll have any trouble tonight. None of the patients are seriously ill, except Ross, and he's stable. It should be a case of plain sailing.'

'Don't worry about a thing. You stay as long as you like at the meeting.'

Just as Mary was about to descend the stairs, she turned and said, 'Oh. . .there is one thing that might happen. And there could be trouble. . . You remember the drunk driver, Noxley?' Alison nodded. 'It's policy here that such people shouldn't be allowed to see their victim.'

'It's the same in England.'

'Well, Noxley has turned up here on many occasions, and last time tried to wheedle his way in by saying he was a relative. Fortunately, my junior nurse saw through him and sent him packing. If I had my way I'd let Noxley see Ross, and show him the terrible suffering his thoughtlessness and selfishness have caused.'

Gritting her teeth, Alison said, 'If Noxley turns up tonight he won't get the better of me. What does he look like?'

'Tall, dark, exceedingly well dressed, but seedy.'

They waved goodbye and Alison walked back towards her office. As she passed one room she saw a young lad with a fractured femur slung on traction. He looked as miserable as sin. So she walked in.

After consulting his chart she said, 'Hello, Lonnin, I'm Miss Maynard. Are you in any pain?'

'We all know who you are. We've all heard! And I'm not in any pain.'

'Your vital signs look steady anyway.' She replaced his chart.

He did not answer. Alison moved nearer to his bedside table. On it was a conch, a handsome pink, brown and creamy shell, with powerful spines running along its crest.

'That's a beautiful shell. Where did you get it?' She was determined to make some sort of contact. From experience she knew that adolescents had a hard time with long-term hospital confinements.

He looked up immediately. 'I found it. It's my lucky shell.' Then he looked down again.

'I'm sure it will bring you luck. If you need anything just press your buzzer.' She had failed to get through to him. And she had other things to do on the ward, so she decided to leave him for the moment. There would be time for him later.

After she had spoken to all the men on traction she strolled back towards her office. But the sound of a man reading aloud in Ross's room alerted her.

It was the boy's father, Mr Kelso. His back

was to the door. Alison stood quietly taking in the scene. Ross had been unconscious for six months now. His face and hands showed signs of deterioration. He was painfully thin and his black eyes were sunken into his head. The Kardex said he was nineteen, but he looked twice that age.

Mr Kelso looked up suddenly as his son's eyes wandered round the room. He rose from the wooden chair slowly, and it scraped over the uncarpeted floor. 'You must be the new charge nurse from England,' he said to Alison.

Alison introduced herself and shook hands. Then she picked up the chart for something to do. She had to get a hold of herself; this patient and his father were in her care now.

The father stood quietly. He was thin too, and his shoulders drooped. 'Have you seen many like my son?'

'Unfortunately, yes, Mr Kelso. And you'd be surprised how many recover, especially when they're young like Ross.' She kept to herself the fact that at six months the possibility of brain damage was very likely.

The father had a sweet smile. 'I think Ross likes your English accent. He's looking at you.' Then he pointed to a famous English actress whose posters were pinned to the wall. 'She's his favourite.'

'I've never thought of myself as that glamorous,' she chuckled.

'Yes, really—look, he's listening to you.'

Alison studied Ross. Certainly his head was turned towards her, but his eyes were distant; they were not focusing.

On the bedside table stood a photograph of a stocky young man with a motorbike. She quivered inwardly.

'Yes, that's Ross before. . .before the accident.'

'Is that motorbike a 650?' enquired Alison.

'How did you guess? Yes, it's my son's pride.'

'I had a boyfriend who loved bikes.'

Mr Kelso's face relaxed into a broad smile. 'Do you hear that, Ross? Miss Maynard must know all about bikes too.'

The boy did not respond.

'Well, I was taught a bit, because he was everlastingly pulling his machines to pieces and rebuilding them.' She laughed, then realised that she hadn't spoken so openly about her fiancé since the accident.

The telephone in her office rang shrilly.

'You must excuse me, Mr Kelso,' she said.

'Yes, certainly, Miss Maynard.' He stepped agilely out of her way.

The phone call proved to be no more than a

wrong number. She replaced the receiver carefully. Gratefully she sat down at the desk and held her head in her hands. Unbidden thoughts of her fiancé crowded into her mind.

He had been known as Mike the Bike because of his passion for motorcycles. And his death had come suddenly, literally out of the darkness of night.

She had been expecting him one evening, but instead of Mike on her doorstep she had been confronted by a young policeman. Alison had found the news of the accident unbelievable, and even more so because the policeman had brought two items from the scene of the crash—a single red rose and an engagement ring in its box. Obviously it would have been a night of proposal.

And when she'd finally reached the hospital ward, and found Mike, lying so still, her heart had almost broken.

He had known that he was about to die and had wanted to put things in order. So he had said, 'It's time for me to ride the big motorbikes in the sky. When you see the white fluffy clouds, you'll know it's me, because that will be the exhaust. Don't be unhappy, and don't mourn for long. And promise me one thing.'

This promise had been the most difficult

Alison had ever made in her life. Mike had made her say that she would marry. Because, true to his generous spirit, he had wanted her to find happiness.

A single tear now trickled down her cheek and passed a chocolate-coloured beauty spot. She brushed the tear away quickly.

And as she lifted her head it was as if she saw through her office door and into the room where the boy Ross was lying. Mike's life had been completely wasted. But the boy was in her care now. He was there like a living exile, not dead but not fully alive.

Taking deep breaths, she steadied herself. And then and there she resolved that he must get better. He must enjoy life to the full. She determined that she would do everything in her power to make this come true.

The door to her office opened slowly, and a man stood there, squinting against the fading evening light. He was tall and his beaver-brown hair was brushed back at the sides. In his charcoal-grey suit he looked sinister.

The man stood motionless for some time. Have I smudged my eye make-up or something? thought Alison. He made her feel uncomfortable.

'Can I help you?' she asked.

He did not answer straight away. Then, 'I'd like to see Ross Kelso first.'

Mary's words sounded a warning in her head. This man was tall, dark, exceedingly well dressed and—oh, yes, definitely seedy. She didn't know when he'd last shaved.

This must be Bill Noxley, the drunken hit-and-run driver who had mown down Ross and left him for dead. Emotion got the better of Alison. The Bill Noxleys of this world were all the same—beneath contempt.

'You're not a relative, are you?' Anger filled her voice.

'No. Why do you ask?' The man continued to stare at her.

'Then you can't see him. I know about you. I've heard your story, and you needn't think that just because I'm new here you can get away with anything.'

'It's obvious you *are* new here.' He spoke with a note of authority. 'What on earth would I want to get away with. . .as you so quaintly put it?'

He had walked a few steps into her office and shut the door behind him. Alison stood up, making the desk act as a barrier between this would-be murderer and herself.

'They should take your licence away! Aren't you ashamed of yourself?'

With two quick strides he was before her, his arms straight and supporting his body as he leaned on her desk, his face only inches away from hers. She was afraid.

'Listen to me, Miss Maynard. I don't know who you think I am, but don't ever criticise my professional standing. I'm Dr Zeke Armstrong, and when I say I want to see one of my patients I want to see him—and right now!'

Her eyes flew open. 'You can't be! You're in New York on a conference. Now listen here, Mr Bill Noxley, I've been warned that you've tried this sort of thing before. So. . .you have a choice: either leave my ward and my patients or I'll call Security.'

It was an ultimatum that she issued to no great avail. The dark man laughed, brushed his long fingers across his blue stubble chin, reached into his breast pocket and withdrew his wallet.

Alison was getting more nervous by the moment.

'I usually only have to produce identification when I pay by cheque.' He thrust his driver's licence before her eyes.

Alison was horrified to see his picture and his name clearly printed—ZENNON ARMSTRONG!

CHAPTER TWO

'I'M SORRY, I thought you were the drunk driver who——' Alison stammered.

He cut in, 'You thought incorrectly and without taking into account all the facts. I might agree with your sentiments about drunk drivers, but as a doctor I wholeheartedly condemn your actions. You behaved emotionally—that's the only way I can put it nicely. And there's no place for emotion in my hospital, certainly not on my ward. Is that clear?'

It was as if she were a first-year nurse all over again. She felt reduced in stature. But not to emotional tears.

'I apologise. But, Dr Armstrong, I was told you were away——'

'Call me Dr Zeke,' he said abruptly.

She could have kicked herself for that mistake.

'I was in New York, now I'm in Hawaii. I gained several hours travelling west on my flight, so I thought I'd put that time to good use and check up on my patients.'

She swallowed and stared at him. He glanced at his wrist-watch. How strange, she thought. His suit and tie and shirt are all executive style, yet he wears a heavy, dull black watch just like a deep-sea diver's.

'I'm tired,' he said abruptly. 'Let's get on. As I said, some time ago, I'll see Ross Kelso first. Bring the file trolley.'

The door to her office jerked open and she saw his dark shape exit rapidly. She knew he was still seething with temper, because his back and shoulders were taut.

Then Mr Kelso stood up to welcome the doctor, holding out his hand and smiling. The gestures of the unconscious boy's father were all Alison would have needed to know for sure that this man was Dr Zeke. No plastic card, no gilt-framed diploma, no white coat or dangling stethoscope could convey the doctor's professional standing as well as the look of the patient's father.

After the usual small talk Zeke Armstrong listened to an exhaustive description of how Ross had eaten his supper, which Mr Kelso fed to him each evening.

'Well, your lad certainly looks very up to date with that spiky hairstyle,' he mused.

'It's wonderful,' explained the father. 'One

of the young nurses cuts and styles it for him. He always likes to be in the fashion.'

'Very New York, I would say. And we always try to do our best for each patient here on 419.' Dr Zeke turned to Alison. 'Don't we, Miss Maynard?'

'Yes, sir,' she agreed.

'I'll make a clinical examination of Ross now.' Zeke continued to stare at her. 'Well, shut the door to the patient's room.'

She was momentarily startled, but soon pulled herself together and rolled back the bedclothes.

Zeke handled the boy's legs gently but firmly. Then he checked the reflexes and spoke calmly to Ross. 'Clench my hand,' he ordered.

Ross rolled his eyes and tried to withdraw his fingers. He was locked in a world of his own. Dr Zeke straightened the bedclothes and replaced the cot side. Turning to Mr Kelso, he said, 'You know, I think he's a little more lively than when I last saw him.'

'That's wonderful!' The father beamed. 'Of course, I see him every day, but you've had time away, and I expect you can see the improvement more clearly.'

If Dr Zeke had told Mr Kelso that he had won the jackpot or a cruise on the *Queen*

Elizabeth, the man could not have looked more pleased.

Dark eyes were burning into Alison again. She wished he would speak rather than just stare. 'Miss Maynard, we ought to make use of the ideas from England. Have you any bright new methods of treating the unconscious?'

His remote look unnerved her. She stammered, 'Music. . .we played their favourite music to them on cassettes.'

He indicated the cassette radio on the bedside table.

'Um. . .a brightly coloured mobile in the room. It helps them to focus. . .' His fingers carelessly touched a mobile of cars hanging above the bed.

She was silenced.

'Nothing else to offer?'

She couldn't think. Dismissively he turned his back to her and spoke to Mr Kelso again.

Once alone with her and in the corridor, he said, 'Are there any patients with particular problems that you think I should see first?'

'No. . . I think everyone is stable and coping well.'

His gaze penetrated so deeply that her eyes prickled. Then the two of them made their way uneventfully through the male side of the ward. But when they turned into the four-bedded room where Lonnin Goddard lay Alison saw her patient restlessly flicking the monkey chain above his bed.

'Who's the new patient?' Dr Zeke asked abruptly. Keeping his eye on the boy, he held out his hand for the file. Mercifully Alison was able to locate it quickly.

'Lonnin Goddard, sir.'

He studied the file, flicked through the sheets of histories and forms with test data, then checked the TPR chart at the bottom of the bed. Satisfied with the written details, he shook Lonnin's hand and introduced himself.

The lad looked decidedly piqued as Dr Zeke checked the weights and pulley system of the traction and eyed the boy's leg, checking the alignment. Alison felt that something disastrous was about to happen, and she would get the blame whatever it was.

'Everything seems to be in order.' Dr Zeke walked around to the boy's side again.

'Yeah,' was the only answer he received.

'Any pain at the fracture site?'

'No. . .'

The wall of silent communication was up, just as it had been with Alison.

'No problems, then?' The doctor was looking concerned.

'Yeah, plenty of problems. I'm in here!' The voice was half shrill, half guttural.

Immediately Dr Zeke took command in an even, low key. 'It's always hard to adjust, especially at first. You've only been in a couple of days.'

'Four days and three nights. And they say it'll be weeks, even a whole year, before the bone is back to normal! I can't take it. I'm used to being outdoors. . .' The young man clamped his teeth together and glared at his leg. A glazed film covered his eyes as he desperately tried to hold back tears.

'Whoever told you that it would take a full year for you to recover has obviously given you the wrong impression. I'm sorry about that.' Dr Zeke gave Alison a crushing look.

She gulped. It was obvious he thought it was her. But as he had embarked on a long discussion with Lonnin it wasn't the time to defend herself.

'In your case, Lonnin, new bone will be laid down at the fracture site within the first week. This is young bone, often called woven bone, because of its irregular pattern. After that mature bone is formed. It takes up a complicated design that will transmit the stresses that you'll put upon your leg when you stand on it.'

Looking at Lonnin's crumpling face, Alison thought Dr Zeke would do better to tell the boy exactly how long he'd be in bed. But then the doctor looked exhausted after his journey.

'I'm not staying in this dump for a whole year!' protested Lonnin.

This is it, thought Alison. A complete crisis, and I've just told Dr Zeke that all was well on the ward.

Dr Zeke placed a calming hand on the boy's shoulder. 'There's no reason to believe that you'll be hospitalised for that length of time. Your type of fracture is uncomplicated enough to take a cast brace. And that means you could be up and about with the brace and crutches in just over a month.'

'A month, you say?' Lonnin's face looked less agitated. 'But I heard a year!'

Dr Zeke cut in deftly, 'It's true that it can take up to twelve months for the fracture to become so completely healed that, in some cases, it's impossible to see the original site of the injury. But you'll be active long before then.'

Then, changing his tone, he asked almost casually, 'Who told you it would take a year, Lonnin?'

'I don't know—I can't remember. All I know

is that it shook me. I'm down to go to the University of Hawaii in the fall.'

'Congratulations.' The doctor looked almost handsome when he smiled. Alison saw a humane intelligence cross his face. It was a pity she was in his black books. 'By the time you start your fresher's year at university you'll be well ahead in your recovery programme.'

Lonnin's rapid breathing had almost regained normal timing, as he sank back into his pillows. 'But I've still got to lie in this bed for weeks yet.'

'You'll have to be patient and give your body the chance it needs.' Dr Zeke sounded a little weary now.

'It's all very well for you to say that! How do you know what it's like? You've never broken your leg or been tied to a bed, I bet.'

He's starting up all over again, thought Alison with dismay.

Dr Zeke's voice was low and steady. 'Most obstetricians have never had a baby, but their patients manage to produce children very frequently. The human race hasn't died out yet.'

Good answer, thought Alison.

And Lonnin laughed, showing his teeth. 'That's funny. But the trouble is I can't sleep.

I'm used to curling up on my side; that's how I always sleep.'

'A lot of patients find that at first,' Zeke explained. 'Would you accept some sleeping tablets just for a few days?'

'Pills? No way.'

'I didn't think so. Then I'll organise some relaxation lessons. The psychologist will come and teach you.'

'Tonight?'

'No, it's very late Friday evening now. But we'll have that organised by Monday, won't we, Miss Maynard?'

'Yes, of course,' Alison replied, making a note on the chart.

'That won't help me over the weekend,' Lonnin moaned.

Dr Zeke stepped towards the locker and bent to study the conch. 'Particularly fine,' he mused. 'May I examine it?'

What was Zeke up to? Alison couldn't fathom it. But the boy seemed slightly distracted.

Zeke's fingers traced over the spines, then probed into the dark oval opening. Alison felt an uneasy tingle slide down her back.

Holding the shell to his ear, Zeke said, 'In ancient Hawaiian times the blowing of the shell was used as a rallying call for warriors.'

He turned to include Alison. 'I can hear the sea in it. Hold it to your ear at night, Lonnin. The rhythmic soothing sound, like the sea, will help to lull you to sleep.'

To both Alison's and Zeke's delight the boy held out his hand eagerly. 'Yes,' he sighed, and lay back again, seemingly lost to the sounds of his conch.

Then Alison felt steel fingers grip her elbow. 'A word outside with you, if I may.'

She was forcefully steered into the corridor. Her heart plummeted. She knew what was coming.

'I thought I asked you if anyone was in need of immediate attention, Miss Maynard? And if my memory serves me right you said, and I quote, "Everyone is stable and coping well". Now young Goddard was not coping. He was in a lot of emotional trouble. I think if I hadn't turned up tonight the night staff would have had a real handful to deal with.'

'I'm sorry. But everyone was all right when I came on duty. Nobody told me of any problems.'

'Nobody told you! Aren't you capable of making a judgement yourself, Miss Maynard?' His brown eyes were disdainful. 'I was expecting a great deal more from a nurse trained at

St Mary's and then at Oswestry. I'm a Thomas man myself.'

Bright colour rose in Alison's face until it felt as if her cheeks were glowing like red hot coals. A Thomas man indeed! You could always tell a Thomas man, but you could never tell a Thomas man anything.

'I've done my level best in the time, Dr Zeke. I don't think you quite understand——'

'I understand that you, like any new member of staff, are under three months' trial as a probationer. My patients must get the best possible treatment, and I shan't think twice about dismissing you if you don't come up to standard.'

She was stunned by his words. Coming to the hospital at a moment's notice, when she was still on holiday getting accustomed to the heat and humidity, had seemed like a good idea at the time.

All her previous first encounters with staff and patients had been heartwarming. Now this man, with his fierce and critical feelings, was making her feel as though she would have done better not to have played the part of Good Samaritan.

A numbness crept through her mind. Why did he stare at her so? Ordinary people usually had pinpoints of light in their eyes that gave them a sparkle and a quality of life. There were no lights now in Dr Zeke's eyes. Fatigue made his eyelids droop, and as he looked at her through narrow slits she couldn't tell what he was thinking.

Abruptly he spoke again. 'And can't you find an appropriate uniform? When I look at you I could be back in England doing my training all over again.'

'I'll change into *your* prescribed style as soon as the dress is given to me.' She sounded curt and she knew it.

'See that it's soon,' he snapped. 'We've already wasted enough time as it is.' For a moment he seemed disorientated as he looked up and down the corridor. Alison thought he swayed on his feet.

'Are you feeling dizzy, Doctor?' She felt concerned.

'What's that you say?' He flicked his dark brown hair out of his eyes. 'I haven't finished seeing all my patients in this room, have I?'

'You have two more to see if you think you're up to it.'

'Two more, and then the women. Right. . .' Again he looked deep into her eyes.

Was he diabetic or something? wondered Alison. Had he missed a meal and upset his insulin count? That might explain his strange behaviour. If it was that, she would forgive him.

The sound of purposeful steps running up the staircase made him look to his left. 'Ah, here's Mrs Amos.' He greeted her like a long-lost relative. 'Now we'll get the decks cleared in no time.'

He was using a charming little boy's voice that would have taken in many women.

Mary stopped in her tracks at the sound of the young doctor's voice. 'You'll overwork yourself one day!' she chided. Then, seeing Alison, she added, 'I see you've met our new angel of mercy.'

'Yes, but things are a bit rickety here——'

'Don't fret yourself,' sighed the older nurse. 'Miss Maynard has done us a real favour. If it hadn't been for her turning up like this, and before she should start her proper duties, then I wouldn't have been able to settle a family problem. As it is, all's well.'

Dr Zeke looked at Alison with a puzzled expression. 'How long have you been here?' he asked.

She checked her fob watch. 'Two and a half hours, sir.'

To her surprise he looked only slightly chastened. 'It seems I owe you an apology. You shouldn't have let me carry on so. You should have spoken up for yourself.'

'I will in future.' Smiling sweetly up at him, she concealed all the turmoil he had created inside.

Dr Zeke strode off, and began talking to another of his patients.

'He's too dedicated by half,' Mary confided. 'But you'll find he's quite a sweetheart really.'

Alison felt sure she'd never think of Zeke Armstrong in exactly that term!

After being thanked again she left the ward. In the changing-room she checked her reflection in the mirror. No, she hadn't smudged her eye make-up. At one point she had thought that was the reason Zeke had stared at her in that strange way.

As she walked towards the lift she could hear the doors banging and opening on the floor above. Kids from the children's wards, she supposed. She toyed with the idea of using the stairs, but the lift arrived immediately.

Stepping into it, she felt the floor wobble uncertainly beneath her feet. She pressed the button for the ground floor. The lift descended, but not for long. After a moment it stopped, then started again. I've got a bad feeling, thought Alison, and crossed her fingers behind her back.

The journey down was interminably slow and accompanied by heavy metal clicks and rasps. Wherever this thing next stops I'm getting out, she thought.

The doors opened. Below her feet she saw that the floor of the lift was not flush with the corridor; it had stopped a good eighteen inches above. Normally, I'd jump and think nothing of it. But too much has already gone wrong today, she thought.

'Stay there—I'll help you down.' That sounded like a very welcome voice.

A young man ran forward, placed his left hand on the door of the lift and held his right hand out for her. 'Take my hand,' he said. At that moment the doors decided to close again, and Alison drew back as they inched together. The man leant heavily on them and sent them crashing back. He grabbed her and pulled her through.

Then she was free and looking up gratefully into his face. He was young, only about twenty-four, she guessed. The same age as herself.

'Thank you,' she gasped. 'I was beginning to think I'd spend the night here going up and down like a yo-yo!'

'No chance,' he laughed. 'Someone would have prised you free, even if all they had to hand was a tin-opener.'

She laughed and felt immediate relief. She noticed that he wore his sandy hair parted at the side and that it flopped over his right temple in a deep wave. There was a calming reassurance about him. But although he smiled she thought there was a hint of sadness behind his eyes.

His voice sounded soft, but it was like that of a man who had suffered innumerable set-backs until at last he accepted and let it all wash over him. His pearl-grey suit was immaculate and blended well with his cream shirt, black tie and black breast-pocket hand-kerchief. A really snappy dresser.

Not wanting to make a fool of herself for the second time that night, she asked if he was a doctor.

'You do my suit great credit! No, I'm a medical salesman. I'd like to have been a doctor, but my brain cells weren't up to it.'

She smiled. His friendly attitude was a reflection of the hospital as she had first known it. Before Dr Zeke.

'Well, I feel I was lucky that you came along when you did.'

He bent to pick up his black leather brief-case. She was scanning the corridor when he straightened.

'Are you looking for something?' he queried.

'No. . . I mean yes, I was looking to see if there was a bus timetable posted somewhere.'

'You don't seem very sure of anything. Is it your first time here? Are you visiting a relative?'

'Actually, I work here. I'm a charge nurse. I started work this evening.'

'No wonder you look lost! And *aloha*.'

'What does that mean?' she asked.

'*Aloha*? It means hello, goodbye, welcome, and often serves as a general endearment. If I'm to be typically Hawaiian I should show you true hospitality and give you a lift home.'

Although she tried to protest, he insisted. Walking towards his car, she thought, he's so gentlemanly, and I feel quite safe with him.

In the car he twisted around to place his briefcase on the back seat. 'Now, where to?'

'It's. . .' The exact address eluded Alison. For the life of her she couldn't remember the name of the street or the apartment buidling. 'This is stupid. . . I can't remember!' and she burst into tears.

'It's not such a problem,' he said gently,

and, taking his pocket handkerchief, he pushed it between her fingers. 'There's no point crying over such a simple thing. Do you live with anyone?'

'I'm staying in my sister's and brother-in-law's flat. They're in Europe for a while.'

'I bet they're on the phone, and we can easily look up the address that way.'

Alison stopped crying. 'You have all the answers.'

'If all problems were as easy to solve as yours, there wouldn't be much heartbreak in the world.'

'I don't know your name.'

'Geoff Renton.' He held out his hand.

'And I'm Alison Maynard.' As they shook hands she felt a quiet warmth from his touch. He was a nice man.

'I'm glad you're not upset any more,' he said. 'When you laugh you remind me of my sister. She had green eyes just like yours.'

Alison suddenly felt that she had become far too wrapped up in her own problems. She had been thinking of nothing but herself. And now Geoff Renton was speaking of his sister in the past tense. Looking into his eyes questioningly seemed to make him nervous, because he dropped his keys and his glance as well.

The black handkerchief lay crumpled in her lap. She picked it up and blew her nose. 'You must think I'm really silly.'

'No, I expect you've just had a bad day. Everyone gets them.'

She sighed. 'I don't think many people make as many bad mistakes as I did this evening. The surgeon on my ward turned up unannounced and I didn't know who he was. I thought he was the drunk driver who'd mown down one of my patients, so I tore him off a strip before he could say who he was.'

'Oh, dear!'

'I wouldn't normally have made such a blunder, but. . .' She went on to tell Geoff about the unconscious boy and how he so closely reminded her of her fiancé. 'And here I am rambling on! Why should I dump it all on you? Especially as you've been so kind already.'

'I'm a good listener. Sometimes that's the best help anyone can give.' He shrugged.

Alison looked down and saw that his black handkerchief looked like a well-worn dust rag. 'I'll wash and iron this before I give it back to you.'

'That's OK. I should have given up wearing black a long time ago.' Swiftly he changed the subject. 'What's the name of your brother-in-law? We ought to look up his address.'

'I remember now.' Alison beamed. 'The apartment block is the Prince Lohian.'

'I know it. Very smart, and just near Waikiki too.'

As Geoff drove Alison asked, 'What branch of medical sales are you in?'

'Medical hardware.'

'Respirators, anaesthetic equipment and those things?'

'No, the actual replacement hardware for the body—artificial joints, knees, hips, ankles, even the little joints of the fingers.' He flexed and straightened his hands. 'And plates, screws and pins. All the things that a surgeon uses to cobble the bones back together.'

'I knew we had something in common.' Alison chuckled. 'My ward is 419. We use a lot of your hardware on our patients.'

Geoff looked very pleased. 'I like to work on the orthopaedic side of the hospital. Mostly you can help patients to get better and go back and lead productive lives. It's not like the progressive neuro-muscular diseases. That's what my mother and sister had. . . Huntington's Chorea. . .'

Shocked into silence, Alison understood. She knew the disease. Usually it affected the young, and they died young too. And it was genetically transmitted.

'I'm sorry,' she said gently. 'Sorry' seemed so inadequate. 'I believe they're doing a lot of research in that field.'

'Yes, the research. There's always the hope.' His voice sounded faint. 'There, I've told you all my troubles too.'

And mine are minor compared to yours, she thought, and bit her lip.

Geoff drove her home by way of the coastal road. As they passed the marina one ship caught her eye. In the night light it looked like a ghostly galleon gently moving on the water, its masts and rigging silhouetted against the deep blue of the sky.

Geoff caught her line of vision. 'You're interested in tall ships, are you?'

'That big one over there is particularly impressive. I bet she looks a majestic sight with all her sails unfurled.'

'There's a funny thing, and not surprising. You've picked out the *Neptune*. She's the fanciest ship you'll see for miles—a windjammer, and several hundred years old. And who knows. . .?' He laughed. 'You may just get the opportunity to sail on her.'

Alison looked puzzled.

'You work on Ward 419. And the *Neptune* belongs to Dr Zeke.'

The surgeon had been furthest from her mind at that point. Alison swallowed hard and grimaced. 'I doubt I'll be among the favoured. Not after tonight, anyway.' Oddly the thought saddened her.

'Don't be so pessimistic! Zeke's a fair man. I've always found him so in business deals. And he's not the sort to bear a grudge.'

Outside her apartment block, she said, 'Thank you for saving what might have been a really black day.' She kissed him lightly on his cheek.

Surprisingly, he looked away quickly and she became aware of a mighty tension that crept throughout his face. It was obvious that this sort of physical contact caused him distress.

To lighten the situation she said softly, 'You've been a good friend to me tonight. I hope we'll remain *friends*.'

Geoff seemed to understand the implication and visibly relaxed. 'I'll see you at the hospital—I'm always popping in and out.'

Inside her kitchen Alison reflected on the awkward way they had said goodbye. And as she sipped a cool orange juice she remembered the sweetness of his smile when he had comforted her. Geoff was a sweet young virgin. But why? Then she remembered the Huntington's Chorea that had affected his family. Maybe he was a carrier of the fatal disease. Maybe the thought of sexual relations and the chance of a child frightened him. And certainly contraception wasn't always one hundred per cent safe.

If this indeed was Geoff's problem she felt sad for him. But she wouldn't give him up as a friend. She didn't feel like embarking on any sort of romantic relationship at the moment. But they might be good for each other in a platonic way.

And she might feel the need for some support, especially working all day with a surgeon like Dr Zeke. If Geoff was a sweet young virgin then Dr Zeke was the opposite. With his brooding dark looks and his magnetic masculinity, he would attract many women.

Alison doubted that Zeke ever spent a night of celibacy!

CHAPTER THREE

THE beach at the Ala Moana was bigger than at Waikiki, or so it seemed to Alison. Bright early morning sunshine had woken her that Saturday morning and she had decided to sunbathe before the intense heat.

Only about half a dozen other people were about, and most of them were far out at sea. Out behind the breakers the surfers were rising and falling on the swell of the ocean. Some lay lazily on their boards, seemingly idling their time away. But one man, all black and as slick as a seal in his wet-suit, sat astride his board. Its nose tipped up out of the water at a cocky angle.

He paddled his board across the ocean and sat astride it again. A restless energy about this man made Alison stare. He studied the waves as they made their steady progression from the ocean and broke into foaming curls nearer the shore. Then he was looking at her, studying her.

She flushed and looked down. And when she looked up again he was still staring at her.

He was so far away that she couldn't make out his features.

Pretending to read a glossy magazine, she stealthily looked his way again. He fascinated her. Not for a moment was he still. A mental and physical restlessness emanated from him.

Above the drumming of the surf, she heard the surfers calling to one another. Their muffled cries of exhilaration as they rode the waves pierced the air. She thought their achievements dazzling.

The surfer in black studied the sea and the way the waves broke. Alison was drawn to him as if by magnetism. At one moment his senses became alert. He watched the approaching hump of water as a cat watched an innocent bird.

The swell was building and building. The surfer turned his board towards the shore and lay down. All the time he looked behind, then as the heave of the wave approached he paddled furiously. The swell reached him and he rose high on the crest.

Kneeling first, then standing upright with his pale feet wide apart, he soared through the surf. With his arms thrown wide apart for balance he could have been some mysterious powerful angel riding the hinterland between the blue heavens and the ocean.

The sight took Alison's breath away, as his whole body shimmered in the sun's glare.

The curl of the wave was huge; the surfer leaned forward and the board shot ahead. Then, as he gave a violent fling of his arms, the board jumped in the air to face the opening in the curl. He crouched low on the board. Suddenly he entered the curl of the crashing wave, and was out of sight. . .nowhere to be seen.

'He's gone!' she cried aloud. She felt a tightness in her chest as if she couldn't breathe. What if he's drowning? she thought.

She was counting the seconds, then unexpectedly he shot through the surf, but fell, unable to regain his balance. The board cartwheeled across the seas with a vicious force. He was gone.

Alison sprang into a standing position and scanned the boiling seas. The board was picked up by another wave and headed towards the shore, towards her.

For what seemed like an interminably long time there was no sign of the surfer, then she saw a head and an arm raised in triumph, waving at her. Without hesitating, she waved back.

Another wave, smaller than the one in which he had ridden the tube, arrived. To her astonishment he lay face down, placed his arms by his sides and with his face out of the water began to kick. The swell took him and soon he was surfing towards her without a board.

She'd never seen anything so brilliant in her life!

It was only moments before he was walking aggressively through the shallow waters. Scooping up his surfboard, he walked purposefully straight towards her.

His body was dripping with water, and his brown eyes sparkled alive as he held out his hand.

'Hello, Alison. This is a much better place for us to meet.'

She was speechless as she automatically shook his large hand. And he continued to hold her hand captive as she stared into the warm brown eyes of Dr Zeke.

'I. . . I. . .didn't recognise you.' She stumbled over her words.

His grin was mischievous. 'That makes twice! But I'd like to apologise for my behaviour last night. I was jet-lagged and edgy, and you were new. I think it's best forgotten. And call me Zeke, please.'

The constriction she felt in her chest and especially around her heart began to relax.

'You were under the ocean for so long that I began to get worried.' She knew her mind and conversation were grasshoppering, but she still found it hard to believe that he was both the surgeon and the surfer in black.

He laid his surfboard on the sand and sat down languidly in front of her. 'Under the ocean was the best place to be. The board was loose and it could have given me a nasty bang on the head.'

She offered him a fruit juice, which he drank in swift short draughts. For a big man he was very graceful, she thought.

Instead of feeling relaxed in his presence, she felt her heart begin to race a little. 'Why do you wear the wet-suit? I would have thought the waters around here would be warm enough.'

'Quite right. You're very observant. I'll show you.' He sprang to his feet and started to pull the suit jacket carefully over his head. As he hunched his shoulders and wriggled his torso and arms, it looked a complicated manoeuvre.

With his torso fully revealed he looked the essence of strength and beauty. His attractive masculine power was only made more sensual by the thick tufting of black hair across his chest.

'Here.' He pointed to several deeply penetrating scratch marks along the side of his chest and arm. 'I didn't want to chance another wipe-out on the coral. It could have re-opened these wounds, and they're healing nicely now.'

'The coral must be razor-sharp!' Alison sounded concerned.

'These scars aren't important; they're only signs of healing.'

'That's a very philosophical way of looking at it.'

His gaze was full and candid. 'It's the best way to view it. Otherwise even small problems can get on top of you, and build up out of all proportion.'

Alison understood.

Again he sat down, this time even nearer to her. He's like a bronzed mariner, she thought. The black waterproof watch that he had slipped off to remove his wet suit lay behind him, seemingly forgotten.

'Don't lose your watch,' she pointed out.

'I won't.' He retrieved it. And that same dreamy, faraway look that she had seen in the office clouded his face.

Reaching out slowly, his forefinger touched her cheekbone just below her birthmark. 'It's natural, not painted on.'

A tingling glow remained on her face even as he withdrew his hand. This was a new sensation to Alison. He was too sensual, too dangerous. She was out of her depth with him and she knew it.

'I didn't realise you had a specific interest in dermatology. I thought your scene was orthopaedics.' She laughed uncertainly.

Zeke smiled to himself and lay flat on his back. Lying in so relaxed a position, he looked perfectly content.

She looked away to the ocean once more.

'What are you watching?' he asked lazily.

Having to think of something quickly, she blurted out, 'The surfers.'

'Why don't you try it some time?'

She had the distinct feeling that he was about to offer to teach her. 'When I'm a bit more settled and my job is going well. I'll concentrate on that first.'

'A wise answer,' he chuckled. 'Make sure you have proper tuition when you learn. Don't go out in the waters just anywhere. The ocean can look deserted, but in some places there are sharks.'

'Thanks for the warning. In the water with that wet-suit on you could be mistaken for a predatory animal.'

With lightning speed he sat up to confront her. 'I'm not Kawelo, you know,' he told her.

She was disturbed by his physical agility, and her green eyes widened. 'Who's that?'

'Hmm, I see you're not familiar with the legend. Some Hawaiians still believe it. Kawelo was a sorcerer. He could change into many disguises, but his favourite was to metamorphose into a shark.'

Alison grimaced.

'His guise never completely left Kawelo, because even in human form he had the gills of a fish and the mouth of a shark at the back of his shoulders. The tail and flukes of the shark were still on his lower body.'

Zeke lowered his voice so that she was forced to lean forward to hear. 'And to hide his animal parts he wore loose-fitting garments. He was artful, too. When he wanted to escape his enemies he took on the forms of other creatures—worms, moths or butterflies.'

'Do you always tell such gory stories?' she queried.

'Seriously, though, Alison, you don't have to believe the legend, but there are sharks about.'

'You, for instance.' She managed to smile.

'Not at all. Look at my back—I've no gills or mouth there.'

His boyish grin made her laugh out loud. She had been fully aware of his body, but she wouldn't like him to know.

Turning his wrist, he consulted his bulky black watch. 'Damn! Is that the time already? I'd like to stay, but I've got to get back to the hospital. Thanks for the juice.'

'I'll see you at work, then.' She waved him goodbye and watched his tall figure stride up the beach and towards the road. Such a strange man, she mused, and so full of weird stories.

Rolling on her back, she remembered how exciting it had been to watch him ride the big waves. He was altogether too exciting. As she looked up at the sky she saw the fluffy white clouds, and thoughts of Mike the Bike flooded her mind. Was it possible that she had forgotten him so quickly in the presence of Zeke? She felt guilt steal through her veins and she rolled over and pushed her face in the sand.

At eight o'clock precisely on Monday morning the staff stood patiently as Mary Amos gave the report in the office. Alison sat on a chair beside her. She had been introduced formally to everyone.

Mary began, 'Ross Kelso had a comfortable night. Very little change in his unconscious state over the weekend. Nurse Roberts, you'll special Ross today, please.'

'Yes, Mrs Amos,' the young nurse replied eagerly.

'Try and get Ross to eat more. And pay special attention to his right elbow; it looked a little red this morning. I'll order a sheepskin pad.' Mary turned to explain to Alison, 'OT make them here.'

Alison made a mental note.

'Ah, Lonnin Goddard!' The whole staff raised their eyes to heaven. 'He has a substitute for a teddy bear now. He uses his conch to cuddle at night. Apparently the sound of the sea lulls him to sleep.'

The last patient on the ward seemed to be causing some concern too. She was Anne-Marie. Alison remembered her as the twenty-year-old who had stepped out from behind a car without looking. She had been knocked down by another car and sustained a fractured pelvis. Now she had a double hip spica plaster of Paris, which meant that she was literally encased from her waist to a distance well down both legs.

Mary looked exasperated. 'The night staff caught Anne-Marie poking a knitting needle down the waist of the plaster cast. Now we all know what can happen if the skin is scratched beneath the plaster. It doesn't breathe, it doesn't heal. And I've seen some nasty sores develop that way.'

After the jobs had been allocated to the staff, Alison was sent to Admin for the paperwork and then to get her new uniforms. Then, back on the ward, she took over the duties for Ross while his nurse went to coffee.

Alone with the boy, Alison pressed her hand to his forehead. He had the greasy skin of an adolescent, and a few angry red spots on his chin that must have hurt when he was being shaved.

'How's that elbow of yours?' She rolled up his pyjama sleeve to inspect the area. 'These hospital sheets of yours are full of starch, and. . .' she drew her fingers over the material. 'These sheets are really rough.'

He made funny tight sounds in his throat as she spoke to him. They were half caught, unintelligible noises.

'Is it time for your TPRs yet?' She looked at his chart. 'Not for a while.' These one-way conversations were odd. However, you never could tell how much the patient was taking in.

Her elbow brushed against some books on his nearby table. 'Let's have a look at these, shall we?'

She glimpsed Zeke, passing by in the corridor outside. His head was down, bent purposefully over a letter written on flimsy airmail paper. He didn't see her.

Turning back to the books, she scanned the titles. 'I might have known this one was here! It's the *Owner's Workshop Model for a Honda Motorbike*.' Ross appeared to watch her lips.

'This book reminds me of an old friend of mine. Shall I read some of the manual to you? It might jog your memory.'

Inside on the first page of the manual she saw familar words. 'I expect you know that the Honda empire was started in a wooden shack in 1947, don't you, Ross?'

Her patient was quiet as she read on page after page. Then she felt a gentle touch and, looking down, saw the boy's hand resting on her arm.

'What do you want, Ross? Shall I go on reading?' Then something made her lean towards him and she whispered, 'My fiancé's life was wasted. Yours mustn't be. Come on, let's see if you can sit up by yourself, instead of just lolling back on those pillows.'

She unhooked the lock of the side rail on the bed and folded it down. Sitting on the bed facing him, she pulled him forward by the shoulders. His body came towards her unsteadily, but his head remained on his pillows.

Placing one hand behind the base of his skull, she spoke firmly. 'Sit up, Ross. Sit up!' He didn't have the control.

But after a while Alison felt some movement in the muscles of his neck. Then momentarily he would hold his head in an unsupported position. She was jubilant at this small success. 'Well done, Ross!'

'Oh, Ross, you're brilliant!' The young nurse specialling him came up to Alison's side.

'I think you're on the way to the road to recovery,' Alison told Ross.

The young nurse added, 'Dr Zeke will be delighted.'

It wasn't until much later that morning that Alison met Zeke. He looked very aloof and professional in his spotless white coat.

'I prefer you in the hospital uniform,' he told her as his frank gaze swept up and down her.

She didn't let his austere manner faze her. She presumed that he preferred to be slightly distant here on the ward.

'I'd like to check up on Ross, if that's convenient,' he said. 'You never know when some small breakthrough might happen, with head injuries.'

He marched straight ahead into the boy's room before Alison had a chance to mention the improvement in head control.

Zeke's examination of the boy was along the same lines as it had been on that fateful first ward-round. But she felt more relaxed about things. She certainly wasn't expecting the reproof that came next.

'His teeth aren't clean, Miss Maynard.'

'We do our best, sir, but it's difficult for us to clean his teeth, especially with his condition.'

'I'm well aware of that.' He took a paper handkerchief from a box on the windowsill and to Alison's horror extracted what looked like a half-chewed bacon rind from between the boy's first and second molars.

'It can't be that difficult to get this free from his teeth if I can do it.' Zeke sounded impatient.

Fortunately for Alison the young nurse spoke up. 'He's just started chewing his toothbrush, Miss Maynard. Usually I give him an apple after breakfast to help clean his teeth, but this morning he refused it.' She hung her head.

Dr Zeke looked at the young nurse. 'So he's

getting a bit awkward, is he? Still, it was a good idea of yours to give him an apple. I think he's in caring hands with you.'

That was uncalled-for, thought Alison resentfully.

Then Zeke put his hand to the boy's forehead. 'Not much change generally. I think I'll move on.'

'Oh, but there *is* a change.' Alison could keep silent no more. 'He's regaining head control.'

'Really, Miss Maynard? Since when? I can find no sign of it today.' His voice cut her. 'I think it would be best if you confined yourself to nursing procedures.'

Alison wasn't going to take this rebuff. She felt it imperative that Ross should start more active physiotherapy if he was to recover. And he had to recover.

Walking past Zeke, she boldly pulled Ross into a sitting position. His body felt like a sack of potatoes and to prove her wrong his head hung back. After some time she heard Zeke drumming his fingers on the bedside rail. 'Hold your head up, Ross,' she urged. Nothing happened.

'You've proved nothing by this, Miss Maynard.' The surgeon sounded terse.

But at the sound Ross lifted his head and

turned towards Zeke. He was at the boy's side in an instant. As he brushed close to Alison she was filled with triumph on behalf of Ross, and annoyance at herself for being edgy.

Zeke's fingers gently probed the muscles in the boy's neck and shoulders. 'Very definite muscle contraction here!' He sounded delighted. Then he took control of the boy and let him sink back into his pillows. 'I'll get Physio to start balance and reflex exercises. In fact, I'll see about it straight away.' And with a curt nod he left the room.

Of all the arrogant, chauvinistic men I've ever met! boiled Alison inwardly. He hadn't bothered to acknowledge that she had been clinically correct. Still, it didn't matter. As long as Ross got his treatment.

Turning to the young nurse, she said, 'You did very well to speak up like that when Dr Zeke tried to criticise our basic nursing procedures.'

'Thanks, Miss Maynard.' The girl looked slightly bewildered. 'Dr Zeke seems strange today. He's not usually snappy.'

Hmm, thought Alison. That man suffers a sea-change far too frequently for my liking, and I don't know why it's always in my presence.

CHAPTER FOUR

'Is IT usual to be giving out bedpans during the evening visiting hours, Miss Maynard?' Zeke's critical eyes bored into her.

Bad timing had meant that she had bumped straight into him outside the sluice. And now she stood before him in her barrier gown and with the offending item in her hands.

She hadn't seen him since yesterday's confrontation about Ross. But it seemed that whenever they met on the wards it was to be ill-fated.

'I'm sorry, sir. But our patients are only human, and this is a call of nature.'

'Who's the bedpan for, anyway?'

'Anne-Marie, your patient with the fractured pelvis.'

'Well, I hope you've got another nurse at hand to help with the lifting. I remember when I applied that plaster for the chastity-type double hip spica it made the whole thing very heavy.'

Alison was surprised that he should be concerned about her back. 'That won't be a problem. Her husband is with her and he's only too willing to help.'

'Even so, it can't be very pleasant for the other patient and her visitors in the same room.' They were standing outside the room now, and Zeke popped his head around the open door.

There he saw old Mrs Rackham lying asleep. She had removed her hearing aid and it was placed on her bedside locker.

'I don't think Mrs Rackham has many visitors,' Alison said quietly.

'Huh—that's nothing for her family to be proud of,' he muttered almost inaudibly.

Alison noticed that his airmail letter was threatening to topple out from his white coat pocket. More to distract him, she said, 'You'll lose that if you're not careful.'

As he looked down the muscles in his face hardened. 'Damn thing,' he growled, and, thrusting it deep within the pocket, he strode off without the courtesy of another word.

After shaking her head incredulously, Alison made her way towards her patient. Anne-Marie and her husband looked quite agitated by this time.

The young husband piped up immediately, 'There's no need for you to stay. I can give it to my wife.'

'I think it would be better if the two of us lifted together.' Alison was adamant. She didn't want any more problems—certainly not a patient falling out of bed and cracking her plaster.

It proved extremely easy to slip the bedpan under Anne-Marie. She was able to hike her body up by pulling on her monkey chain.

'Just leave the barrier gown with me, please,' the husband said eagerly. 'You see, I can easily manage, and I can take it away when she's finished.' And, as if to confirm his point, 'I've done it before.'

Alison agreed. She was pleased to see him so attentive. Support like that would help Anne-Marie to recover more quickly.

In the office Mary Amos was leaning on her desk with her hand over her eyes.

'What's the matter?' asked Alison.

The older charge nurse sighed. 'I've needed the patience of a saint with Lonnin Goddard all week! And now today nothing is right. I wonder he hasn't complained that the sun's rising too early for his liking.'

'There's one on every ward,' agreed Alison. She chuckled, and then asked, 'Is he sleeping all right?'

'Yes, that conch idea that Dr Zeke told him about seems to be doing the trick. But Lonnin has taken a dislike to his psychologist. Never mind; as long as he's sleeping the relaxation techniques aren't all that important.'

'Everyone seems on edge today.' Alison sat down in front of Mary. 'Even Dr Zeke. He didn't think the ward was being run very efficiently when he caught me giving a bedpan to Anne-Marie a moment ago.'

'This is becoming a habit with our Anne-Marie!' Mary looked puzzled. 'Still, if her husband doesn't mind lending a hand I suppose it saves wear and tear on our backs.'

Alison was curious to know more about Zeke, so she followed up her line of thought. 'But is Dr Zeke usually so critical?'

'No, but now you come to mention it, he has been a bit tense lately.' Mary leaned back in her chair. 'I used to know him when he was a teenager, just before he went to England to do his medical training. He was much more full of life and fun then.'

A buzzer from one of the patients sounded urgently. Checking her deck of lights, Mary exclaimed, 'Oh, no, not Lonnin Goddard again! I suppose he's feeling a bit left out. I had to tell him this morning that his family couldn't visit until later this evening, so I expect he wants some attention.'

'I'll go and check him out,' offered Alison goodnaturedly.

But once she saw Lonnin as white as his sheets, she had the distinct feeling that something serious had happened. 'What's the problem?' she asked gently.

'There's a funny feeling in my leg and it's making noises,' he faltered as he waved his fingertips above the site of his fracture.

Alison felt a qualm run through her. 'Have you got any pain?'

'When it clicks it's. . .ugh. . .horrible!'

'When does it feel like this?' She kept the alarm out of her voice.

'When I do that muscle contract-relax technique that the psychologist taught me. I was feeling a bit upset, so I thought I'd give it a try. I should have stuck to my conch.'

Very gingerly Alison placed her hand over the fracture site. 'Try a very slight quads contraction,' she told him. The quads were a bulky set of four muscles running at the front of the thigh.

Lonnin looked sceptical. 'Just try once,' she encouraged, and as he did so she not only heard a click but she also felt a grinding movement.

'Oh, there it goes again!' gasped the boy, and clamped his hand over his mouth.

Alison wanted to clarify exactly what had caused the problem. 'You've been doing these exercises with your physiotherapist haven't you Lonnin?'

'Yes, but I'm only supposed to do them gently for her. I think it was the psychologist's fault. He made me do them very hard.'

'Just rest that leg completely for the moment and I'll get Dr Zeke to take a look.'

Alison left a very worried-looking young boy. Mary was still in conference with the family, so she paged Dr Zeke from the phone in the corridor.

He answered almost immediately and in a bright voice. She introduced herself and said that there could be a problem with Lonnin.

Immediately he sighed. 'Are you sure the trouble isn't in his head? I've just had a long conversation with one of the radiographers, and she told me that Lonnin almost screamed the department down when he was having his immediate post-trauma X-ray. Are you sure he's not pulling your leg?'

Alison decided not to rise to this. 'I don't think he's pulling *my* leg when I can hear clicking and I can feel grinding when he does a quads contraction.'

She heard his sudden intake of breath. 'Now how the hell did that happen?'

'I believe the psychologist has been a bit over-enthusiatic with the relaxation technique, and included the fractured leg too vigorously.'

'I'll be up straight away.' And she heard the receiver click back into place.

Zeke was calm and reassuring as he examined Lonnin.

'Is it something terrible?' asked the boy, raking his fingers through his hair.

'It's a very slight setback in your rehabilitation.' Zeke chose his words carefully. Alison noticed that he didn't mention that the new bone had broken down. This information would surely put Lonnin straight into panic stations.

Zeke continued, 'The leg just needs a couple of days' absolute rest, and then I think we can proceed as normal.'

Mary was still in conference with the family, so Zeke led Alison into the small ward kitchen. 'Congratulations! That was an excellent piece of clinical detective work. Especially with a boy like Lonnin, who's complained non-stop ever since his admission. Something serious like that could easily have been overlooked.'

'It was just good nursing; anyone else would have done the same.'

For a moment he looked at her in that

strange remote way. Then she saw the corners of his mouth tug into a smile. 'Patients can let even the best nurse down at times. Ross chewed his breakfast to the front of his teeth just as I examined him. And then Anne-Marie had a call of nature when all the ward work should have been done.'

A brightness animated his eyes. 'I feel I ought to redeem myself with you, Alison. I know you're working a split shift tomorrow and your afternoon is free. Do you like animals?'

This is a curious conversation, she thought. 'Yes, I love all animals.'

'Good. I think you'd enjoy a visit to Sea Life Park. I have a working lunch with Admin, but I'll be free at two, so I'll meet you outside the hospital main entrance then.'

His invitation was so unexpected that she hesitated before answering. And as she gazed into his warm eyes she decided he was devastatingly handsome.

'I think you'll enjoy the dolphins and the killer whale,' he added.

'Yes, thank you, I'd love to come.'

At the door he turned and she thought she glimpsed a hint of mischief in his face. 'Just be sure to wear something casual and cool—it might be hot for your fair English skin. A cotton T-shirt and skirt would be suitable.'

Mary was free when Alison walked back into the office, and she was as shocked about Lonnin as Zeke had been. They discussed the matter for some time. Then Alison remembered that Mary had said that Zeke used to be full of fun, so she brought up the subject again.

'I don't know why he's so serious about everything now,' Mary puzzled. 'But then I've only worked with him for six months. Before that I was on the mainland for some years, so I've no idea what happened to the Armstrong family in that time.'

There was some mystery in Zeke's background, Alison felt sure of that. It intrigued her. Perhaps she'd find out more during her afternoon at Sea World.

'I hope I didn't keep you waiting long.' Zeke's voice pierced her consciousness before she saw him. She had been sitting on one of the wooden benches outside the hospital.

He looked very Hawaiian. His hair was freshly washed and shone in the harsh sunlight, and he wore tailored white jeans and a bright shirt patterened with reds, yellows and blacks.

'I wouldn't have recognised you if it hadn't been for your voice,' she said. He looked so casual, not at all the distinguished surgeon or the black angel of the foaming waves.

'I tried to cut the meeting short, but someone kept on talking,' he explained.

'I was enjoying the breeze here. I didn't mind waiting.'

Zeke guided her to his sports car. It was the colour of burnt sand, with black bumpers—very impressive.

Opening the car door, he said, 'You haven't got any back problems, have you?'

What a strange question, she thought. 'No.'

'These cars are so low-slung that you can get your back out just climbing in.'

Alison wondered if that was his only reason for asking. She slid in and covered her knees with her skirt.

'I love watching the dolphins,' he began as they drove off. 'They're such intelligent creatures. The mothers make devoted parents.'

She hadn't imagined Zeke as a family man, and she studied his profile as he concentrated on manoeuvring through the traffic. His chin was strong and his angular bone-structure made him look very dashing. He was a powerful male, which made it all the more fascinating to glimpse the softer side of him.

At the park he said, 'Let's see the *Essex* first. That's an old three-masted sailing ship which is permanently berthed here. It's in the pool where the killer whales are kept.'

They sat in the open air in a structure built like a Greek amphitheatre. The mountains rose behind and to one side, while the sea stretched to their left.

The killer whale was enormous. The wake it created in the pool rose and fell several feet as the gigantic black and white creature leapt and performed turns in the air.

Like the children and everyone else in the crowd, Alison and Zeke gasped as the whale shot high out of the water to take a fish from a girl suspended on a narrow balcony strutting out from the ship's mast. As the creature crashed down into the blue waters a shimmering spray flew through the air. Alison was so enchanted with the sight at this point that she didn't notice a mischievous smile stealing across Zeke's face.

After this show he said, 'Let's go to the Dolphinarium now. It's cosier there.'

This stadium was designed like a flying saucer on stilts. Here the seats were much closer to the smaller round pool.

'It's best if we sit right up at the front.' Zeke

ushered Alison into the first row. 'Are you enjoying it here so far?'

'Yes, it's brilliant,' she enthused.

Dolphins and keepers entered the stadium, and the two beautiful creatures dived, then jumped through the air, excited at the prospect of play.

Zeke's face suddenly creased into a broad grin. 'Watch this!'

The dolphins jumped over a yellow and red bar suspended from the ceiling. They leapt so high and landed so joyously that the spray sheered up like a wall and drenched Alison. She was soaked from head to toe and so was Zeke.

'I'm so sorry,' he said, but with the laughter scarcely concealed from his voice. 'I've got a handkerchief somewhere.' He thrust his hand deep into his trouser pocket.

It became clear to Alison immediately she looked down. Her sopping wet white T-shirt now fully revealed her breasts and nipples. He had set the whole scene up deliberately.

'I suppose this is your idea of water sports with women!' She was flaming mad and could feel herself blushing.

'Me? He tried unsuccessfully to sound innocent. 'No. . . But if you'd like me to teach you how to surf any time I'm very willing.'

He held out his handkerchief and in anger she snatched it. Mopping up was an embarrassing situation, especially as he offered several times to help her. Even though he was soaked himself, he didn't seem the least put out. And when she gave back his handkerchief, which she had made a great show of wringing out like a dirty dishcloth, she was acutely aware of his muscled thighs straining against his wet trousers.

But she nearly lost her temper altogether when he leaned over and whispered softly, 'Now I understand why those statues of partially nude women on the Acropolis in Ancient Greece were so popular. . . It was the wet drapery effect!'

Folding her arms firmly over her breasts, she said, 'Well, this show is definitely over!'

At which he threw back his head and laughed helplessly. And when at last he had finished he gazed steadfastly into her eyes with a deep and wholesome admiration. He confused and surprised her at every turn. And now he looked different, more relaxed than she had ever seen him before and years younger.

Later they walked around the different aquariums, and when he slipped his arm through hers she didn't withdraw. The warmth of his skin against hers felt right.

'We've a little more time before we're both needed back at the hospital,' he said as they walked towards his car in the car park. 'Would you help me with some shopping?'

Alison had enjoyed her afternoon so much that she didn't want it to end. 'Of course. What do you need to buy?'

'Baby toys.'

'I didn't know you had any children.' She was shocked.

'I haven't—not yet. But the idea is fun, don't you think?'

She blushed.

'My sister is pregnant,' Zeke added smoothly, seeing her confusion. 'I believe there are some good shops in the Ala Moana.'

In the shopping centre it was refreshingly cool. They easily found a shop especially for children's toys.

Alison was secretly pleased to be helping him. 'What kind of toy did you have in mind?' She pointed to a green dragon with red eyes.

But he only raised his eyebrows.

'Do you know if she's having a boy or a girl?'

'My sister had the ultrasound scan, but she opted not to be told about the sex.'

'I think I'd feel the same way. It would only spoil the surprise.'

He looked at her with such a tender expression that she felt drawn to him, but lowered her eyelashes.

She found a pile of rabbits on another shelf and absently pulled their ears through her fingers, just as she had done with her own pet ones when she was a child.

'I think I like the idea of these rabbits in their natural fawn colours.' Zeke picked out a large one. 'What about this one with the crooked smile?'

'Perfect.' She took the toy from him and examined it. 'Oh, yes, the eyes are button ones, not those on metal stalks, and it's made well.'

'This one will do for a start, then,' he laughed, and took it to the assistant.

All too soon they were back outside the hospital in the car park. 'Thank you for a lovely afternoon,' said Alison. 'I enjoyed everything.'

'I'm glad,' he said simply, and, stealing his arm about her shoulders, drew her close and kissed her lightly on the lips.

Instinctively she pressed her lips against his in response. The scent of his aftershave, and his closeness, drove all other feelings of commonsense from her mind. She wanted to kiss him more deeply, and she was about to, when he drew back.

His fingertips brushed gently down her right cheek and that old remote expression replaced the tenderness in his eyes. 'I mustn't forget my brown rabbit,' he said carefully, and turned away to retrieve his parcel from the car.

'Dr Zeke!' called a middle-aged hospital postman who was pushing a mail cart. 'Here's a letter for you. It came by the second post today.' He held out a blue airmail envelope.

It crinkled as Zeke took it. Alison saw how the young surgeon's mouth twitched and how the muscles in his neck stood out with tension.

'Thanks—I've been expecting it.' He held the letter behind his back out of Alison's sight. And when the man had left he spoke in the most formal, constrained manner. 'I mustn't make you late for work, Alison. It would never do to keep patients waiting.'

Before she could reply, he had left and was disappearing quickly into the main entrance. She was left alone and dumbfounded. The delicious sensation of his kiss faded immediately. Really she knew nothing about him, and her own willingness to kiss him so openly and in so public a place now filled her with shame.

This man was able to inflame the most passionate feelings within her body. And she had forgotten how vulnerable she was. She must just have been seeking a quick replacement for Mike. That was her only explanation for her wanting to kiss Zeke.

And airmail letters seemed to throw him into a state of split personality. She would do well to give him a wide berth from now on.

Zeke did not put in an appearance on the ward that night. But he was never far from Alison's thoughts. She was still thinking about his enigmatic ways at the bus stop after work when a bright voice called out to her.

'You can't take the bus when you can ride with me!'

'Geoff! My knight errant of the lift shaft!'

He leaned over and opened the door, and she slid in gratefully. 'I'm glad you remembered me that way,' he told her. 'I rather like that name.'

She was pleased to see him, and told him so.

'How are you getting along with Dr Zeke

now that you've been on the ward a couple of days?'

'Fine,' she lied, and turned the conversation around to his work.

'I've got to go to Nevada tomorrow. I'll be there for a while.' He sounded a little depressed. 'But we could have a good time tonight, if you'd like to come to a club?'

She agreed, because she wanted to be with Geoff for his last night, and she had a day off following.

The club proved to be in Chinatown. This part of the city was brilliantly aglow in the darkening night. Neon, argon and mercury lights advertised clubs, restaurants and shops of all kinds. Dragons climbed to the sky, lanterns dangled and the streets were crowded with people.

After parking the car Geoff said, 'Stick close to me—I don't want anyone to get the idea you're on your own. These streets at night aren't for the loner.'

'Might I get shanghaied, then?'

Geoff was serious. 'In more ways than one.' He kept his arm tightly around her waist as they entered the club. It seemed ordinary enough; people were drinking and dancing.

They did not stay in this area, but moved upstairs. A man looking rather like a gangster from the Al Capone era greeted Geoff as a long-lost friend and took them into a corridor from which they were several doors. He took them through one into a crowded room.

Alison looked about. 'Everyone's gambling! she exclaimed.

'It's an exciting way to play.' He laughed.

'I'm not sure I approve.' She looked around, stunned.

'You will when you've won a few times.'

The scene before her fascinated her. Money in the form of brightly coloured stacks of chips changed hands at an alarming rate. The people were intense, and so ordinary-looking. She could have passed them on the street, or treated them in the hospital.

Geoff bought chips and gave some to her. 'Oh, I'll just watch you to start,' she said. 'How much is here?'

His answer startled her. It was more than a month's wages.

The dealer stood before the wheel and called, 'Place your bets!'

Chips covered the numbers until they were almost out of sight. Then the wheel whirled dizzingly fast, numbers and colours blurring into circles. The ball dropped, bounced up and dropped again.

'If only it had stayed down the first time!' Geoff bit out. His chips were gone.

Alison was disturbed by the chips in her hand. They made her feel uncomfortable. 'Here, you use them.'

'You'll be lucky for me.' He blew on them and placed them. Again the wheel spun, the ball dropped and his chips were lost. 'Lady Luck just wasn't riding for me tonight.'

'It's awfully stuffy in here,' Alison complained.

'OK, we'll go out.' He sounded depressed. When they were out on the street, he said, 'You didn't like it much in there, did you?'

'It frightens me. All that money, and the House wins most of it.'

'That's the odds. But you can win at times as well.'

'I just don't like the idea of gambling.'

Geoff laughed. 'Everyone does it. The stock market—that's just a casino for the rich. Then there are the lotteries, and in England you have the football pools.'

'Yes, my granny used to do the pools.'

'Exactly—everyone bets in one way or another. And life is a gamble too. Does everyone get one hundred per cent better in hospital?'

'No.' She thought of Mike.

'Is every baby born perfectly normal?' Geoff's voice was low. 'When I gamble, I don't do it for myself. I send the money for the research into Huntington's Chorea. They need it, and perhaps a cure can be found.'

Alison was reminded of his sister and his mother. The odds had been stacked against them, and they had died. She looked at Geoff, and his face was white with fear. A shocking thought entered her mind.

'Are you a carrier for Huntington's, Geoff?'

He looked away, 'I don't know.'

'You could have genetic counselling. You could have the test, then you'd know for sure.'

'If I don't have the test then I can live in hope.'

'But you might be negative. You might not be a carrier at all.'

'I can't bring myself to take the test.' He sounded so dispirited. 'It's the one thing I can't gamble on.'

Alison saw his eyes wide and white with the burden he carried. She had no answer for him; there was nothing to say. She linked her arm through his; it was a small enough gesture, but all the comfort she could give.

A dark man came out of a shop doorway clutching a brown-paper parcel. He was tall and dressed in a black shirt and faded denims. His head was down, and he walked quickly and almost bumped into Alison.

'I'm sorry,' she said automatically.

His dark face, illuminated by the flashing neon, glared down at her. She knew that dark disturbing look. It belonged to Zeke.

No! Anyone but Zeke, thought Alison, and dug her fingers into Geoff's arm. Geoff surfaced out of his gloom. He hadn't noticed the surgeon.

But the surgeon had recognised them all right, and Alison was sure his disquieting expression meant that there would be some repercussions on the ward!

CHAPTER FIVE

CONFLICT with Zeke came swiftly. Alison had just entered the hospital building on her next working day, when he detained her in a quiet part of the corridor.

'Are you aware that some parts of the city can be dangerous, Alison?' he demanded.

She didn't like the authoritative tone in his voice, but before she could answer he went on.

'Were you out gambling with Renton on Friday night? Do you know that gambling is illegal here in America, except in some states like Nevada?'

She was staggered. She hadn't realised that. But, thinking back, they had been ushered into a secluded part of the night club.

Having to think quickly, she defended herself. 'We were enjoying a night out dancing, that's all.'

He raised a dark eyebrow, that left her in no doubt that he thought she was lying. 'Have it your own way,' he muttered disdainfully. 'But those streets can be unsavoury.'

'I hardly think so—after all, you were there too.'

His eyes narrowed. 'I was picking up a Chinese take-away meal from a restaurant I know very well. In fact, the owner is one of my patients. I'm known in that district; I would never come to any harm. You, on the other hand, were out with someone barely out of his adolescence. I suggest you try a *man* as an escort next time.'

Alison was furious that Zeke should try to assume so commanding a role in her life. And she bridled at the implication that Geoff was inadequate in any way.

How dared Zeke ever criticise Geoff when he obviously knew nothing about his tragic background?

Her emotions got the better of her as she said, 'For your information, I *was* with a man that night, and a very satisfactory one at that! Now, if you'll excuse me, I'm needed on the ward.'

She left him abruptly, and fumed all the way to the changing-rooms. Zeke had no right to be so intrusive! She had implied that she had slept with Geoff, but she didn't care what Zeke thought. And now she was much more concerned for Geoff. Right now he was in Nevada where the gambling was legal, and in his state goodness knew what that would lead to.

As the weeks passed the hostility that had sprung up between Zeke and Alison subsided. He became aloof and withdrawn; it was as if he was wrestling with a deep internal problem.

Alison watched his change of mood curiously. But she was more concerned about Geoff. He had promised to keep in touch. However, since he had left for Nevada she had heard nothing.

But there were even more pressing problems needing her attention, and they were on the ward.

Ross Kelso had received several weeks of intensive rehabilitation in the department. There had been some physical improvement. He had a little more head and shoulder control, and now could sit with his back unsupported for short periods.

Unfortunately, he had started to yell and scream at times. It was his reaction to all the stimulation. This distressed all the other patients, the whole of the nursing staff and, worst, his poor father.

One morning Alison was in charge. They were short-staffed and particularly busy, so she ordered the nurse specialling Ross to help with the general bed-baths.

Leaving the door to her office open, so that she could hear the phone if it rang, she sat with Ross herself. And, picking up the workshop manual on motorbikes, she said, 'I'm going to read to you again—I think it might jog your memory. You try and concentrate.' Propping the book open in front of him, and with her back to the open door, she showed him a page illustrating different tools.

'Can you recognise any of these? Look here's an open-ended spanner, here's a ring spanner, this is a crosshead screwdriver and here's a tongue wrench.'

She pointed each out in turn. The boy appeared to be looking, but she couldn't be sure if anything was entering his consciousness.

As she read out the different names, she was reminded of the times when she would help Mike with his motorbikes. The memory made her sad.

But she pulled herself together and said, 'When I helped my boyfriend in his garage I used to hand the tools to him, just as a nurse would hand instruments to a surgeon in the OR. My boyfriend used to laugh, and he called it playing "Dr Mechanic".'

Alison couldn't be sure, but she thought she saw a ghost of a smile cross Ross's lips. She became excited, and continued more loudly.

'Can you remember some of the things that sound like the different parts of the body?' She flicked quickly through the pages of the manual. 'Here. . .torque arm nuts, brake shoes, breather pipe to the battery and gland nut?'

Ross seemed to be looking at her more intently. 'Come on, try and remember,' she urged.

She was so intent that she didn't notice anyone standing behind, until the boy looked over her shoulder.

Zeke's deep voice was filled with warmth. 'I think this game is helping you, Ross. This is an excellent idea of yours, Miss Maynard.'

Alison was startled. How long had Zeke been there? How much of the conversation had he heard? Being unaware of his presence, she might have revealed parts of her past that she would have preferred to keep from him.

'Gland nuts and tongue wrenches. . .do you know those, Ross?' Zeke spoke to the boy with a deep compassion in his voice. 'Squeeze my hand hard if those names ring any bells.'

He had put his large hand around the boy's

wasted fingers. He repeated the words again, very deliberately. Then Zeke's eyes lit up and Alison saw the fingers curl around the surgeon's.

'Excellent, Ross!' Zeke sounded as ecstatic as Alison felt.

After a few more encouraging words Zeke ushered Alison into the corridor.

'Was that a voluntary response or just a reflex?' She couldn't keep the joy out of her voice.

'Voluntary, I hope, We must keep our fingers crossed. It's over six months since Ross's accident, and this is a critical time.'

Zeke gazed down at her, and there was great tenderness in his eyes. Their shared experience with the boy had started to forge a bond between them. As yet, it was loose, but all the same Alison felt it growing.

Then she noticed the great black circles around Zeke's eyes. 'You look desperately tired. Have you been operating all night?'

'Yes, unfortunately.' He sighed. 'A crazy young man decided to play on a building site, and he fell through a roof. It was as well that he's died. He had extensive head injuries too.'

'Go and sit in the office while I organise some breakfast for you,' she told him. 'You look as though you haven't eaten for ages.'

'Great idea,' he replied gratefully. 'But coffee and biscuits will have to do—I'm due in clinic.'

In the ward kitchen Alison hurried to prepare the tray. But as she went into the office Zeke was walking out.

'Surely it can't be that urgent?' she protested. 'Have your coffee first.'

He grinned as he said, 'The Gods must be on our side today. I've just taken a call from X-Ray, and Lonnin Goddard's leg is fit for a cast brace. So I've arranged for him to be fitted tomorrow afternoon. I'm about to give him the good news.'

'But have your break now—Lonnin can wait for a few more minutes.'

'From what I've heard from the rest of the poor patients in Lonnin's room, they'd like him to have the information now. It'll stop his complaints for a day or two at least!'

Alison shook her head. Zeke was one of the most considerate surgeons she'd ever met.

Sitting down at her desk, she went back to some paperwork. Lonnin would probably talk for an eternity. But when she heard the whoops of excitement and then Zeke's footsteps she knew the surgeon had manged to make it a brief consultation.

'Jubilation all round! It sounds as if the good news went down a treat.'

Zeke laughed and slumped on to the chair in front of her. She poured his coffee, then pushed a plate of biscuits in front of him.

'Lonnin and the other patients are over the moon, as you can hear,' he told her as he gulped his hot drink. 'I thought he'd jump out of bed, traction and all!'

'More seriously, though,' said Alison reflectively, 'I'll tell everyone on the ward to keep a good weather eye on that lad. He's liable to try and walk as soon as the cast brace is on.'

'Good thinking. He's not to get up walking until the plaster is good and dry. I've known some patients to be over-enthusiastic and within days the new bone has broken down because the cast wasn't given time to set and give the required support.'

Zeke pulled his legs under the chair and sat forward, looking intently at Alison. 'When I passed Anne-Marie's room she looked very restless. Have you noticed anything unusual about her?'

Putting down her biscuit, she replied, 'No, but she told me the other day that she was bored and missed her friends from work.'

'And, no doubt, that very attentive young

husband of hers.' Then, almost to himself, 'She's damn lucky to have so caring a spouse.'

The ugly set of his mouth as he spoke this last sentence made Alison wonder if he was remembering some bitter old experience. But she had no time to think on, because he stood up agilely. 'I'd better get on with that clinic. Thanks for the coffee. I'd rather have had a leisurely breakfast. . .perhaps we can arrange that another time.'

'Of course,' she replied.

But his mischievous grin as he said goodbye made her come to the conclusion that breakfast with him wasn't meant to be on the ward. He had set her pulse racing, and, to be honest, she enjoyed the experience.

In the afternoon Alison made the drugs round with a junior nurse.

'More drugs!' scowled Lonnin, as she handed the small plastic cup to him.

'They're only vitamins and minerals to help your leg to heal,' she countered.

'When I'm up with the cast brace I'll rattle,' he complained.

'Very funny! But unlikely, I think.'

'Good food and a good night's rest, that's all I need to get well.'

She gave Lonnin a withering look, but he went on all the same.

'The food is uneatable here, and no one can sleep at night now.'

'All your meals are particularly well prepared and presented. As for the noise at night, I'm sure it's only temporary. The young boy has been seriously injured and he isn't at all well.'

'Well, when I'm up on crutches I'm going to give him a piece of my mind,' he shot.

'You'll do no such thing, Lonnin. You'll have the good grace to leave Ross alone and not add to his suffering.' She was hot and flushed with her protective outburst.

'Sorry, Miss Maynard,' he muttered. 'It gets on everyone's nerves, though.'

'I'm sure. But Ross doesn't do it on purpose.'

'Yes, yes,' he muttered.

'Haven't you got a book to read to take your mind off things, Lonnin?' Alison went on.

He brightened visibly. 'Yes, Dad bought me the textbooks for my introductory courses at university.'

'That's a good idea. You'll be streets ahead of everyone else.' As Alison returned to the drugs trolley she wondered if Lonnin would ever grow up.

* * *

The evening was still quite brilliant from the rays of the setting sun when Frank Kelso trudged on to the ward. Alison watched him through her open office door. She decided to have a talk with him.

He was bending over Ross. 'That's right, son, sleep quietly now,' he was saying.

'Would you like a cup of coffee, Mr Kelso?'

'That would be lovely. I haven't had anything since lunchtime. I've been that busy with the garage that I've hardly had time to think.'

She organised the coffee and a plate of sandwiches, and when the junior nurse placed them on her desk she thanked the girl and said to the father, 'There's been a slight improvement with Ross.' She told him how Ross had squeezed Zeke's hand after hearing about the parts of the motorbike that had names like those of parts of the body.

Mr Kelso was overjoyed at the news, and his eyes misted over. 'Wonderful!' he sighed. 'That's a lovely story and a sure piece of hope to hang on to.' He looked her steadily in the face. 'I knew it was a good omen when Mrs Amos said you were coming.'

Alison's heart was touched by his faith. She only hoped that it wasn't misplaced.

Mr Kelso stared down at his cup again. 'Has Ross been crying out very badly at night?'

'He wasn't so bad last night.' She tried to sound comforting. The blue-black veins stood out like knots on the back of his hands; she thought he suffered even more than his son.

'I don't understand it,' he muttered. 'All this scientific knowledge about the body baffles me. I thought if Ross was to start on more exercise he was getting better. But then they say you've got to get worse before you get better.'

'It's not always the case,' Alison replied. 'Ross, I think, is just reacting to the changes around him. The physios are very patient with him. He's taken an aversion to the ice treatment and some of the stretching and reflex exercises.'

'What's all that supposed to do?' His voice sounded aimless.

'By stimulating all your son's senses, like touch, sight and sound, they hope to bombard his nervous system and somehow get him going again. A lot of the techniques are new, and no one fully understands the complete workings of the brain. But we're learning all the time.'

'Dr Zeke knows what he's doing. I trust him to do the best for Ross.'

'Yes, he's one of the best.'

Then the father spoke quickly and more strongly. 'It was hard when his mother left us. But I've done everything for the boy. They say that men can't be as good as the natural mother, but I say no. I've done everything just as well and better than some women, except bear him.'

'You've done everything you could for Ross,' Alison commended. 'You can only do your best.'

She felt she had not been much help to Mr Kelso, but he thanked her with great dignity for the tea and sandwiches and the talk.

'Look at me!' cried Lonnin. He was standing at one end of the corridor, the physiotherapist at his side. The cast brace had been applied successfully several days ago.

Alison walked towards them. 'Well, let's see you in action.'

Lonnin concentrated hard, looked at his feet, and then, at the physio's instruction, gingerly placed his crutches forward and stepped up to them. He did this several times with great determination.

'Excellent, Lonnin.' Then to the physio Alison said, 'He's not quite steady enough to be walking on his own yet, is he?'

'No. But he can walk on the ward, just short distances and always with someone.'

Lonnin looked tired, his hands shaking from gripping the crutches with such force. 'V for victory and for vertical. That's the best position. After lying down for so many weeks, I'm really on my way now,' he said.

Both the physio and Alison agreed that he looked worn out, and after a bit of coaxing they made him sit down in his chair next to his bed.

'Look at these knee hinges, Miss Maynard. They're clamped into place with jubilee clips.' Lonnin indicated them through the slit in his pyjama bottoms, which Alison had made for him with a series of safety pins.

'It's a wonderful piece of engineering,' she agreed. 'Now you have a rest.'

After lunch Ross was restless. He would not settle and began to grizzle and cry. Visitors for the afternoon session were almost due, so Mary Amos asked Alison if she could sit with him as he responded better to her than to anyone else.

She held her hand to his forehead. He had no high temperature, but he was fidgety and kept knocking her hand away when she tried to brush his hair out of his eyes. Try as she could, it was proving impossible to settle him.

'Here's a drink, Ross,' she coaxed. 'This is fresh orange juice—it's good for you.' She had shut the door to his room to muffle the noise. With her back to the door now and bending closely over her patient she did not notice the door open.

'Pipe down! Your screeching is driving everyone insane!'

Alison was so startled that she jumped, and so did Ross. The orange juice spilled all over his face and on to his bedclothes.

'Lonnin Goddard! How dare you come in here interrupting treatment?' She pinned back the side rails so that Ross was safe and turned fiercely to face the intruder.

CHAPTER SIX

'I ORDERED you never to come in here, Lonnin!' Alison snapped. 'Now you've upset Ross even more!'

Ross had started to whimper, and Alison was torn between tearing Lonnin off a strip and soothing Ross, for he might erupt into a howling session at any moment.

'Just get out of here Lonnin, now!'

But Lonnin only stood and stared. He said nothing and did nothing. He only looked at Ross.

'What are you waiting for, Lonnin? And I thought you weren't allowed up without an escort.'

Alison's words fell on deaf ears. The boy on crutches continued to stare at Ross lying in the cot.

'Lonnin, do you hear me?' Alison had almost lost patience.

In a little voice, half shocked, half pathetic, Lonnin answered, 'He's in a bad way, isn't he? I didn't realise. And he's so thin—how old is he?'

Her immediate response would have been to shut Lonnin up and march him away. But she remembered what Mary Amos had said about Bill Noxley: the shock of actually seeing Ross might stop him from drunk driving. Now here was Lonnin, who had never had a thought for anyone but himself, actually enquiring about a fellow patient. She decided to let him stay.

'Ross is about the same age as you. And be careful what you say in front of him. He might look unconscious, but he may understand everything.'

'Oh, sorry. . .' He looked down at his leg in the cast brace. 'I can walk; at least I'll be going home soon. What about him?'

'He's not as lucky as you. Only time will tell.'

'Doesn't he have any visitors?'

'Not in the afternoons. . . Now that's enough. I'm walking you back to bed.'

Lonnin was shocked into silence, and there were no outbursts from him on the way back to his chair.

He'll be discharged soon, thought Alison, but Ross will be staying. She returned to Ross and washed his face and gave him a clean pyjama top. He was docile and not as uncooperative as he had been earlier.

There was a knock on the door. 'Come in,' she called. 'Lonnin! I thought I said to stay——'

'It's all right. My brother's walked with me.' Lonnin fished inside his jacket top and pulled out his conch. 'Take it, Miss Maynard.' He stood precariously with the shell held out in one hand, balancing his weight on his uninjured leg. 'It helped me to sleep. I thought. . .well, if it's of any use to Ross. . . I'm just lending it, mind. I want it back when he's better.'

The youth's gesture amazed Alison. This must have been the one selfless action she had seen from him.

'That's very considerate of you. We'll give it a try.'

Lonnin turned and walked away with his head down. His brother spoke to him, but he did not answer. It was often from the most difficult patients that surprises came.

A serious change came over Lonnin after this episode. He asked if he could visit and talk to Ross in the afternoons. Mary and Alison agreed that this would be good for both boys.

One time Alison was on her way to change a dressing when she heard Lonnin giving a fully detailed account.

'When the reactionary swelling had subsided they put the cast brace on. They say it'll be on for five to six weeks, depending on X-rays at the time.'

And another time she heard, 'The axis of the knee joint doesn't keep still. It moves when the knee moves, so when they put the brace on they make the axis at some point at the lower end of the femur—some bony point called the tubercle.'

She shook her head and tried to stifle a laugh as she went back to the office.

Inside the office door she came face to face with Zeke. She would have thought he was lurking there in so silent a way. Immediately he placed his index finger across his lips to keep her from speaking. Then Alison realised that he was listening to Lonnin's one-way conversation with Ross.

Zeke's whole face creased with laughter. 'It's the funniest thing. . . Ross will hear the whole of Lonnin's life history at this rate!'

'Ah, but he means well.' Alison chuckled with Zeke. 'But wouldn't it be just great if Ross woke up and said, "Shut up, Lonnin, you're boring the socks off me"?'

Zeke slipped his arm around her shoulder and kicked the door closed. He was still in his theatre greens and the smell of anaesthetic lingered about him. All the same, this close contact made her heart pound.

'Seriously, though, that was a brilliant idea of yours to let Lonnin see Ross and take in the whole situation after his outburst the other day. That was an excellent piece of psychological rehab.'

'Any good nurse would have done the same.' Her lips trembled a little. He still had his arm about her.

His free hand tilted her chin higher so that she could not look away. 'But you're not *any* good nurse.'

Gazing into his steadfast brown eyes fringed with sooty lashes made her heart pound more and her head spin. He was beginning to rule her body and her mind too.

Mary strode innocently into the office, then coughed discreetly. Alison drew quickly out of Zeke's arms, a fierce blush staining her cheeks.

But the surgeon wasn't fazed in the least. 'I was congratulating Alison on working a minor miracle with Lonnin,' he told Mary. 'Now all we want is a major one for Ross.'

'And that's what it will be when it comes,' agreed Mary.

Zeke excused himself, saying he had to

lecture the physios, and the two women were left together.

'I think there's medical magic in the air, Alison,' Mary smiled knowingly. 'Zeke looks more relaxed and happy. He's almost as bright as the young man I knew years ago.'

Alison blushed even more deeply, but secretly she was pleased.

Alison was looking at her watch that evening and yawning in her office. She had been on split shift today and for some reason she felt particularly tired.

The telephone buzzed. 'Ward 419, Miss Maynard speaking.'

'It's Frank Kelso here.' He sounded dispirited. 'I've got a rush job on here at the garage, and I don't think I'll be able to feed Ross tonight.' It was the first time Alison had known Frank not to turn up, but she understood. 'Is it OK if I pop along later?'

'Of course. And don't worry, Ross has been very good today. He's quiet and hasn't been trying to eat his toothbrush.'

A faint laugh came down the telephone. 'Well, that's something, I suppose. Thanks, Miss Maynard.'

Alison walked into the room where Ross lay and told the nurse.

'I don't mind feeding him at all, Miss Maynard. He was as good as gold at teatime. Just like my baby brother, and he ate all his coconut cake.'

'Did he?' Alison queried. 'I thought he didn't like coconut much.'

Through the boy's window she looked down on the car park outside. She stood staring. On the opposite side of the car park there was a heavy motorbike. It caught her eye. It gleamed in the sunlight, chrome and white, and its huge wing mirrors on either side of its handlebars reflected the sun with a gold brilliance.

'There's a bike down there that you'd like, Ross,' she said. She thought, there's a bike Mike would have liked too.

The nurse came to her side. 'Yes, that's a beauty. I've never seen anything like that before.' She shrugged. 'If Ross was my boy-friend I don't think I'd like him to ride it, though. Look how he's ended up.'

Alison cautioned the nurse silently, then walked smartly back to her office and shut the door. Then she heard voices and a soft knock.

'Come in.'

'It's only me, Miss Maynard.'

'Why, Mr Kelso! We weren't expecting you,' she began.

The tired man walked slowly towards her. 'I thought, if I couldn't spare a few moments for my boy—well, what had it come to? I've come straight from the shop floor. Hope you don't mind.'

'Not at all.' He was in his overalls and a few oil marks were smeared down his trousers. He smelt of barrier cream, the type that Mike always used before he worked on his machines. He had said it protected his hands and the dirt was easier to wash off afterwards.

'I can work through the night on that job—I've done it before. Anyway, what else have I got to do, stuck in that garage all on my own?'

Frank went in to Ross and Alison closed the door quietly behind him. The white bike in the car park, the smell of the grease and the barrier cream assulated all her senses.

She felt she was back in the hospital by Mike's bed. That terrible night. Why did the memories have to crowd back? Why did they come? Couldn't she be left in peace?

Then a loud retort, like a gun firing. She made for her desk. Her legs were shaking, and she had to sit down. Now, more than at any time since Mike's death, she felt his very presence. Quivering inwardly, she swallowed hard and blew her nose in a tissue. The door burst open.

'Whatever is it?' she cried.

'Dirty spark plug! Dirty spark plug!' Frank Kelso gasped. 'He said dirty——'

Alison was on her feet instantly and through the door, Frank at her heels. She knew the boy Ross must have flickered into some state of consciousness. Would it last?

Ross lay with his eyes wide and his hand across his brow. His expression was one of bewilderment.

Alison put her hand to his wrist to feel his pulse. It was strong but fast. His pupils were normal, although the whites of his eyes showed all around the irises.

'You're quite safe, Ross,' she said gently. 'You had an accident and you're in hospital. It's all right now. You've regained consciousness.'

'Dad!' called the boy. 'Where's my father?'

'Here. Here I am. Oh, it's all right now!'

Alison saw the tears filling the father's eyes.

'I don't understand. What happened? Why are so many people here?' The boy tried to sit up. 'I'm as stiff as a board—how long have I been here?'

'Since the week before Christmas, over half a year now,' his father explained.

'That's nonsense!' protested Ross. 'Why, it's only yesterday I had my birthday.'

'It's midsummer now. Look outside.' Alison pointed through the window.

Ross was incredulous. 'How can it be?' He looked from one to the other.

Alison said, 'We'll get Dr Zeke to see you. Apart from loss of memory, I don't think there's much wrong that can't be cured.' She ran to her office and dialled the switchboard. 'Page Dr Zeke—now!'

After a few agonisingly long rings she recognised Zeke's voice, tired but very willing. She blurted out the news.

'I'll be there right away.' She heard the receiver fall on to its stand with a clatter.

The young nurse explained the events to Alison. 'It was that bike, Miss Maynard—you know, the bike that we were looking at earlier. It backfired.'

'It was that bang that roused my son,' Frank Kelso interjected.

For some unknown reason Alison wanted to know if the nurse had seen who was riding the chrome and white machine. It seemed inappropriate to ask.

Footsteps sounded along the corridor; they were light and quick. Then they slowed and Zeke walked composedly into the room. Holding out his hand, he greeted his patient. 'Nice to speak to you at last, Ross.'

The boy made an attempt to push himself up on one elbow, then shook Zeke's hand.

'How do you feel?' asked Zeke.

'I'm not sure, Doctor.' His voice was uncertain. 'I'm very stiff all over.'

'You've been asleep for eight months—unconscious. It's not surprising that you've temporarily lost the suppleness of your limbs. It'll return.'

'Eight months? Whatever's happened at the garage?' demanded the boy.

'Don't worry about that now,' reassured Zeke. 'Lie back and let me examine you.'

With a little help from Alison and the nurse, Ross lay down while Zeke examined his eyes, his heart and his reflexes. It took some time, because Zeke was thorough and methodical. Then he stood erect and smiled. 'You'll do, Ross. Do you remember anything about the accident?'

'The last thing I remember was my bike breaking down. I had to get off to see to it. . . It was awkward with my helmet on, so I took it off. . . Then. . .then. . . I don't know what happened. Now I'm in here.' Ross lay with his mouth open as if to form some word, but he did not go on.

They all waited in silence around the bed.

'And don't you recall any more than that, Ross?'

The boy shook his head.

Zeke continued, 'We'll be keeping an eye on you. I'll have a word with your father outside for a couple of minutes and then he can come back.'

The boy still looked stunned as Alison, Zeke and Mr Kelso congregated in the corridor. But his father gave Ross a wink and he settled back on his pillows.

Zeke was delighted. 'It looks very good, Mr Kelso. As you saw, I've done a cursory examination, and as far as I can tell your lad's going to be fine. We'll be sending him down to Rehabilitation for a thorough neurological examination, then we'll know how to progress.

Mr Kelso shook Zeke's hand vigorously, finding it hard to say much at that moment because of his overwhleming feelings. Then he returned to Ross.

Alison walked down the corridor with Zeke. 'I'm glad I hadn't gone home; I might have missed all the excitement.' A sparkle played in his eyes.

'Ross woke up at just the right time,' she added. 'Frank was getting dreadfully depressed.'

Something inside began to sag, and she suddenly felt very tired.

Zeke bent close and said gently, 'You look all in yourself, Alison. I'll drive you home—just meet me in the main corridor by the entrance.'

She thanked him and returned to her office.

When Ross was settled and dozing, Frank came to her again. 'That's the end of a perfect day,' he said. Then he corrected himself. 'Oh, no, I've still got that job at the garage. But I won't mind tackling that now.'

Alison was curious. 'In all the confusion I never heard exactly how he woke up.'

Frank leaned back in his chair. 'I thought early on something was up. He was responding almost naturally to sounds, then a great bang came outside his window. I felt as if I should see something. . .but no, nothing. I stood up to get a closer look at Ross's eyes. . .and this spark plug here. . .' he pulled an old spark plug from his trouser pocket '. . .gave me a sharp pain as I leaned over the bed. It was sticking into my thigh. Then I remembered you. . .'

Alison sat speechless.

'Yes, it was your words, Miss Maynard. You said that in rehabilitation they tried to bombard all the senses. So I thought. . .smell.

Smelling salts. Ross had cocked his ear to the backfire of the motorbike, so I pushed this old spark plug right under his nose. I don't know why I did it—I just did. It must have acted like smelling salts, because he said. . .' He couldn't go on straight away, '"Dirty spark plug," and he woke up.'

Alison took the old spark plug from Frank's shaking hand. It had black sooty deposits on it. She held it to her nose. 'Phew, it's such a pungent odour! That was a brilliant idea.'

'I don't think I'd ever have thought of it if it hadn't been for what you'd told me. . . I'm going to keep this spark plug. I'm going to make a little frame for it and hang it in the garage. Does that sound silly?'

'No—exactly right. After all, it was the spark of life that brought Ross back.'

'Yes, "the spark of life",' Frank repeated, and wiped his hand across his eyes. Then he stared at Alison. She couldn't think why she saw fear in him now.

'Ross will wake up again in the morning, won't he? He won't slip back into the coma while he's asleep or anything awful like that?'

'That's very unlikely. He was fully conscious just now, and in control of all his faculties; he has a little amnesia—no, he won't drift away again.'

After a little more reassurance Frank left, and Alison saw that it was time for the night staff to arrive. They were jubilant, but pushed her on her way home, saying she looked exhausted.

There was no one in the main corridor downstairs. She went to the front door and looked out. Zeke's car was there; he hadn't forgotten.

Peering through the descending gloom of the dusk, she searched for the motorbike. Suddenly it became imperative that she find the owner.

She should tell him about his good deed. She should thank him. But there was no bike in the car park. She felt thwarted. The desk clerk was reading a paperback; she might have seen the rider. Alison would ask.

'Excuse me,' she began, 'did you see a motorcyclist come into the hospital this evening?'

The woman stared at her as if she was asking for the moon. 'No, I don't think so.'

'Nobody dressed in leathers, wearing a crash helmet or carrying one?'

'Definitely no one like that.' She went back to her reading.

Maybe the man would be here again tomorrow, thought Alison. She would look for him then.

Zeke walked briskly into the foyer. He was wearing a blue suit and an open-necked shirt. His tie was missing.

'You're quite ready, then?' he asked.

'Yes.' She made an effort to look up and smile; her mind was so preoccupied about the motorcyclist.

In the car he said, 'You're miles away, Alison.'

'I'm just tired. It's nothing.'

'You're worn out. All the excitement, I bet.' He sounded concerned. His voice was soft and compelling. 'I suppose you missed supper this evening?'

Alison hadn't given it a thought.

'I'll cook in the galley. A seafood omelette. . .how does that sound?'

'I don't think I could manage all that,' she said lamely.

'Tea and toast, then? When I was a student, that's what my nursing friends virtually lived on.'

'Lovely.' How many nurses had he known? Lots, she thought reluctantly.

At the harbour the docked ships were alight and gently moving on the waters. Zeke guided her aboard and she heard the deck groan beneath her feet.

'I'll go first,' he said. 'The stairs are steep

and a bit awkward if you're not used to them.' He went ahead and she took his hand. He was warm, and, looking into her face, she noticed how long and curvy his eyelashes were.

'Sit in the saloon while I fix us something in the galley,' he told her.

Everywhere below decks was cramped. At least, not one cubic inch of space appeared to go to waste. Alison sat on a small settee built into the side of the ship. It was made of dark wood and soft leather.

Immediately in front was a low table and on the opposite side a desk covered with charts. Shelves filled with books behind a protective rail were above the handsome desk.

Alison looked about anxiously. She could just see Zeke moving about the galley. He had taken off his jacket and was in his shirt with the sleeves rolled up. He looked every inch the master of his vessel.

Someone was staring. She felt a pair of critical eyes upon her. Zeke was busy. No one else was about. She looked from right to left. There was definitely a presence in this saloon with her. But where? She began to feel uneasy and a tightness caught at the throat. Then the slightest of movements made her look up, straight into a pair of amber eyes.

CHAPTER SEVEN

THE amber eyes with black ovoid pupils contemplated her with open interest.

'Oh, a cat!' gasped Alison.

Zeke had the kettle boiling, and the hubble of the water and the hiss of the steam made him deaf to her.

Alison wondered why she hadn't noticed the cat before. It was jet black with a delicate pink nose and deep nostrils. From its lofty hideaway it glided down on to the desk and sat with its tail curled around its front paws.

This cat had a black head, black front legs, and the upper part of its body was totally black. But, as if it wore a jumper and balaclava helmet, its lower half was pure white.

Alison beamed. 'You're very beautiful, whoever you are.'

The cat rubbed itself along her legs. Back and forth she rubbed. It was as if she sensed the turmoil Alison had felt on the wards. Alison put down her fingertips for the cat to sniff.

'So you've already met my mistress.' Zeke stood there with the tray.

She looked up suddenly. 'Is she your mistress? Yes, I see she is.'

'Mistress of the ship, the crew and me.'

'What's her name?'

'She's got a silly name for a magnificent creature—Jumper. That's what everyone calls her, and that's what she answers to.'

'Because she looks as if she's wearing a polo-neck jumper that's still covering her head?'

'Yes.' He laughed, and his eyes rested on the cat. He looked very relaxed here.

'Does she stay on board all the time?' Alison wondered.

'Mostly. And she's always aboard when we set to sea. In the old log-book of the *Neptune* there are entries about a ship's cat. So I'm doubly pleased to have her aboard.'

Zeke handed her a mug of tea and the buttered toast. Alison supposed there would be a crew aboard a large vessel like this. 'Do you have many crew?' she asked absently.

'Just a skeleton one.'

'What else, for an orthopaedic surgeon?' She laughed, and met his gaze. Somehow he made her feel uncomfortable. She bit into a piece of toast and he sat down close to her side. The hot tea was delicious, but it made her tired. Her eyes were heavier now, and such a weight.

'Are you feeling quite well, Alison?'

It was as if all her energy had drifted away. 'The day was so hectic.'

'But a good day for all that, surely?'

She could not reply at first. Her mind was filled with Ross and the recovery, and most of all now that tangible, insinuating presence of Mike. If she had bumped into him in the hospital corridor she would not have been surprised.

She began to cry, slowly at first. Then the tears trickled down, and she let them. They flowed freely, as if for the first time since Mike's accident. She put down her tea and toast, and buried her face in both hands, trying to muffle the sobs that had started and stuck in her throat.

'Have I upset you? Tell me how.'

She was aware of the deep voice close to her ear, and the strong arm around her that was enfolding her to his chest. But thoughts of Mike and the dreadful waste of his life were uppermost in her mind.

Zeke held her closer and rocked her. His chest was a refuge, warm and reassuring in its strength. Still Alison cried on, wetting his shirt so that the thick dark hair of his chest was clearly visible. He was speaking, but she did not hear.

Then his voice touched her consciousness. 'Aren't you glad Ross is better?'

'Of course,' she stammered. 'It's just that he reminded me of my fiancé—he died in a motorbike accident. I am pleased, oh, so pleased you can't imagine. It was so important to me that Ross should get well, and now. . . How silly I am, crying all over your shirt like this!'

She felt his breathing, regular, deep and rhythmic. 'I see,' he said slowly. 'And you loved your fiancé very much, didn't you?'

'Yes. . .' She burst into a fresh paroxysm of sobbing.

'Shh. . .' Zeke stroked her head. He was deep in thought. 'I don't think you've grieved for your fiancé, not really grieved, until tonight. I think it's been a great weight inside your heart. It's out now. Let it go. Then you'll find you can rest.'

She snuggled close to Zeke's chest and cried. And as he soothed her with long strokes down her back she felt the release of all the tension that had lain so long in her heart.

She spoke at last; she felt she wanted to

explain. 'He was so good to me, so considerate. The last thing he said was that I should have fun and that I ought to marry. . .'

'He truly loved you, then. I'm sure he'd be upset if you didn't eventually marry.'

Alison sat up and brushed the tears away, then bent over her handbag and found a handkerchief.

'Tonight. . .' she blew her nose '. . .tonight I was sure he was near—I mean physically near. You know something. . .'

'Go on,' Zeke encouraged.

'It sounds ridiculous.' She told him about the motorcycle that she and the nurse had seen, and how Frank Kelso had said that a bike's backfiring had woken Ross. 'I believed it was my fiancé on that motorbike.'

Zeke held her closer and spoke slowly and with conviction. 'I don't think that sounds silly at all. Especially in a hospital, you can feel strange presences at times. There are many things that simply can't be explained.'

'You're very understanding,' she said quietly.

'We all have to grieve, sooner or later. It's important. You can't end a chapter of your life properly and go on to the next if you don't.' There was an odd tone to his voice, as if he was addressing himself. And, snuggled close to him, Alison couldn't see the odd constrained look in his eyes.

She relaxed her head on his shoulder. It felt so right in this man's arms. In this position she felt secure and protected, as if no harm could ever come to her.

Zeke took her home and kissed her with an infinite sweetness when he said goodbye. She felt very close to him then, as if he had touched her very soul.

That night she dreamed. And in her dream she was on the beach. The sea and sand and palm trees were bright and illuminated by the midday sun, but the sky was a night sky filled with clouds.

Alison sat on the beach, motionless, like a spectator. In the night sky she saw Mike riding the motorcyle, tearing up and round the clouds as if he was motor-scrambling.

Then he dived to earth, and the bike was roaring and shaking like a space craft. He was being battered and shaken by the earth's atmosphere.

She saw him crouch low on the bike to decrease the resistance of the re-entry, his hair forced flat against his head. The roar grew louder; the machine was shaking so much that his image began to blur. In her dream state Alison sat transfixed, her heart bursting, her body immobile as if set in concrete. She was powerless.

Then on the sea she saw the black silhouette of a surfer shooting along with the white waves, and, though she peered and screwed up her eyes, she could not see who he was, for the surf engulfed him.

From then on she could not tell if it was Mike in the surf or the surfer on the white bike; they changed from one to another. It was an eerie metamorphosis that frightened her because she could not understand.

Then Mike plunged into the ocean. Only then was she able to move, and she jumped up and ran to the sea crying wildly.

But Mike was gone and only the surfer remained. He travelled to shore on the boiling waves, and when he arrived in the shallows he took her hand so gently that she forgot everything. Her anguish over Mike was dispelled as if by a charm. She felt only warm gentleness from the dark surfer, and she was glad.

Alison remembered nothing of this dream when she awoke. She just felt warm beneath the bedcovers, and a new feeling of contentment emanated from her bones. Not wishing to disturb this calm, she spent the rest of the day pottering around the flat.

But on Sunday she awoke early, and it was as if she was filled with a new zest for life. Taking her bikini and her beach towel, she took the first bus that came along and with a feeling of adventure stayed on it until she came to a part of the coast that she had never seen before.

A single brown jeep was parked near the sands, but she hardly noticed. No one was on the sands but herself.

After an invigorating swim she ran back to her towel and lay flat on her back with her arms outstretched, glorying in the salty tang of a mild breeze.

A shadow came between her and the sun, and she looked up, startled.

'Have you come for a surfing lesson?'

'Zeke! I didn't know you were here.'

He was laughing down at her. 'I'm sure you didn't. I only came here by chance myself.'

Remembering her night of confessions to him, she felt embarrasssed. Had she made a fool of herself? And was he only being polite when he'd kissed her goodnight? But now as she looked into his eyes she saw only tenderness.

He squatted down beside her. 'This is the perfect time to learn the noble art of surfing.'

'Me? I couldn't swan up and down your big rollers, as you call them.'

Shielding her eyes against the sun, she surveyed him. He was very casual in the bright light of early morning, with his hair falling down over his forehead. He wore baggy Bermuda shorts, exotically patterned with green and black streaks.

'Are you admiring my bumps?' he asked wickedly.

Alison didn't know where to look next. 'I wasn't. . .'

He pointed to patches of grey hard skin on his insteps and knees. 'They're caused from continuous surfing, where my body grips the board.'

'Obviously,' she answered, although she hadn't noticed them before.

'Hawaii is often known as the home of surfing. Captain Cook reported natives surfing in what he thought were canoes in the late eighteenth century. There's a fairly gentle swell this morning, just right for teaching.'

Alison looked far out to sea. She didn't want to make a fool of herself, particularly not in front of Zeke.

'Don't be nervous. We won't start with anything you can't manage. We'll get going in the soup first.'

She was confused. 'What soup? Mock turtle, bird's nest or. . .'

His eyes sparkled even more and he laughed with his mouth wide open. 'You're good for me, Alison. . .more good than you know. . . The soup is the white water that's left after the wave has broken. We'll be near the shore. The water won't come up much above your waist.'

'I'll give it a try, then.' She managed to sound confident. 'In the soup. . .'

'We'll start on dry land, just to give you the feel of the surfboard.' Zeke turned the white surfboard over and unslotted the tail fin, which he laid to one side.

'I'll show you the basic positions. Then you try. Lying. . .' He lay face down on the board. 'From here you can use your arms to paddle. To get to the standing position you go through kneeling.'

She watched as he knelt on all fours and pushed with his hands and legs into the upright position. 'Right, now you try.' His smile was inviting.

By this time Alison was eager. She lay on the board. 'The surface is rough!' She sounded surprised.

'If it was varnished highly there'd be a good chance of aquaplaning. The water would form a film between your feet and the top of the board, and it would be as slippery as if you were ice-skating.'

'Like skidding in a car on a slippery, wet road?'

'Exactly. So I've roughened the top with wax.'

She knelt on the board as he had done, then stood up. It shifted beneath her feet, and she automatically raised one arm for balance.

'Good reflexes.' He grinned. 'Now bend down, use your knees and keep your back straight.'

'You sound like Sister Tutor schooling us to avoid back strain!'

'Well, I'm a surfer tutor this morning. And you can strain a back just as easily on the high seas on top of a board as you can lifting a heavy patient.'

Alison tried, and it seemed easy enough. And after more practice catching pebbles that Zeke threw he said, 'Having mastered dry land, let's go for the wet stuff.'

She stepped off her platform and watched as his strong hands slotted the fin back into place, then they set off for the water's edge together.

As she waded into the oncoming rush of small waves she felt a movement between her legs, and, looking down, she saw the waters teeming with little fish. Silver darts swam around and between her thighs. She cried out.

'What's the matter?' Zeke put the board in the water and it bobbed up and down. 'They're just little fish.' He laughed.

'They startled me, that's all.' She was afraid he would think her a baby.

He bent to scoop one from the water, held it in his cupped hands and stared down. It thrashed about. Then he lowered it gently into the sea and it swam away. He watched it intently. 'She's happy now. Now she's back with her own kind in her own environment. It wouldn't have been kind to keep her, even though she was beautiful.'

Alison felt he was talking of something or someone else.

Alison practised lying on the board and paddling it about. Waves were breaking constantly, and Zeke stood behind her and pushed the board forward as the wave came under her.

Listening hard to his shouted instructions, she paddled madly, then felt the wave lift the board and she was off. It was a short first ride to the sands, but all the same very exciting.

She felt full of adventure and was eager to try to stand. But on her first attempt the board stalled and she was catapulted unceremoniously over the back and into the sea.

Firm hands held her and pulled her from the brine. 'You'll find your point of balance with practice,' Zeke told her.

She loved the excitement of the ocean, and more especially the closeness and physicality with Zeke.

He brushed drops of salt water from the dial of his black watch. 'I've got to get back soon,' he said. 'But I won't leave you to surf alone.'

She looked disappointed.

He caught her expression and said, 'We could just get in one ride out in the real place.' He gestured with his chin beyond the break. She felt his hand in the small of her back, and her pulse raced. She longed to be on the seas with him.

'Do you think I could?'

'Tandem with me? Yes, I'm sure.' His eyes were bright, his smile mischievous.

And what harm could come to me? she thought. No harm at all. It was as if she had nothing to fear when she was with him.

Zeke lay face down on the board with his legs apart. 'You kneel at the back.' He waved with one hand.

'Between your legs?' She was incredulous and half alarmed at such intimate contact.

'There's no other way. Unless you lie on top of me, or me on top of you. Someone has got to paddle us out, and I'll have to use both arms.'

She gave him a look as if to say that she didn't quite believe him.

'Come on, then!' he yelled impatiently. 'Time and tide and all that. And in this case it applies even to a beautiful woman like you.'

The command in his voice made her slide quickly on to the board and between his outstretched legs.

'Kneel down and catch hold of the rails here at the side.'

The board wobbled as she did, and her heart lurched as her knees touched his wet flesh.

'That's my girl,' he flung over his shoulder, and struck out for a place behind the break. He paddled evenly and relentlessly, resting only as a wave broke over them, washing both their bodies with its foam.

Alison had a clear view of his back. On either side of his spine his well-defined muscles contracted and relaxed rhythmically. They looked rock-hard. She marvelled at the beauty and strength of him. . .the powerful contours of his buttocks and his massive hamstring muscles at the back of his thighs.

They were far out at sea when Zeke stopped and swung his legs forward to sit up. As his skin brushed past hers she felt her whole body tingle alive.

He swivelled round to face her. She felt his warm breath on his cheek, he was so near.

'Here we are, "outside" at last.' He was panting slightly from his efforts. 'Now all we have to do is select a wave.'

'Select one?' It sounded as if they were choosing a punnet of ripe strawberries at the supermarket.

'We'll watch the sets of waves as they roll in, then I'll know how we should ride home.'

'Won't any wave do?'

'Probably. But you can always encounter a rogue. Sit astride your board for now.'

Sitting astride wasn't as comfortable as it might have been. Her skimpy bikini cut into her, and now she understood why Zeke wore his baggies.

'How do I know I'm not with a rogue right now on this surfboard?' she asked, half curious, half teasing.

'A rogue indeed!' His face creased with mischief. Then he was serious. 'I've never ridden the seas with a woman until you, now. And I don't believe I'll ever do the same with another.'

'That's hard to believe, considering your mistress lives on board the *Neptune* with you.'

His eyes became suddenly narrow, sharp and penetrating. Alison was a little taken aback at this change.

'Your mistress. . .your beautiful black and white cat, Jumper. She lives on the windjammer with you. . .'

'Ah, my feline lady. . .' His taut muscles relaxed and he nodded slowly with a gentle smile.

Then an idea flashed across his mind and she saw a glint in his deep brown eyes. 'You *will* be the only woman ever to ride the surf with me like this, but, to remind me of your cheek, young lady, I'm going to commission some artwork for this surfboard.'

She couldn't fathom him, but she was bursting with curiosity all the same.

His voice was low. 'I'm going to have a portrait of Jumper painted on this board. And every time I look at it, it'll remind me of this time with you.'

'Should I be flattered?' Alison said uncertainly.

A crooked smile was all he gave for an answer. Then he pushed an unruly tendril of hair off her forehead.

His hairy chest was soaked in the scud of

the ocean. Here and there dried crystals of salt stuck to him, giving him a white sheen. The sun was behind him and in the clear light she could see that his eyes were not pure brown but flecked with dashes of yellow and blue.

His pupils grew bigger. They were so hypnotic that she could have fallen right in. His mouth was warm and firm as his lips found hers. He pulled her close, caressing her neck and shoulders.

There was something deliciously enticing in the way his fingers travelled slowly to her breasts and stroked her nipples into taut buds. On and downward his hand trailed, sending a liquid fire through her veins.

Then his hand rested between her thighs and aroused her further. She kissed his mouth, and eyes and cheeks. Breathing hard now, he pulled her close, almost crushing the breath from her.

He groaned, then turned with a mighty effort to watch the waves. 'It's too difficult to keep balance out here. Unfortunately this isn't the place for high passion.'

She felt lost to him again. And he had that remoteness about him. After a moment she spoke quietly. 'How exactly shall we surf in tandem?'

It was as if she'd pulled him back to the

present. He answered matter-of-factly, then grinned.

'Toboggan style. I'll sit with my legs forward and steer with them and my arms on the rails, and you take up the same position behind me. But grip your legs very tight to mine and hold round my waist.'

Alison felt the rise of the huge roller, then they were lifted several feet above the rest of the dark sea and hurled forward.

It was like motorbiking. She held on to his body and gripped him for dear life. Then sea was crashing all about them; their speed increased and they were almost flying in the rush.

It was as if she was suspended in time and space. Huddled against the powerful back of this man, she felt the thrill and exuberance she had seen on the faces of the dedicated surfers.

Zooming along so close to the water's surface, Alison, with her heart in her throat, felt as if they were travelling at least at seventy miles per hour, or knots, or whatever. The power of the wave subsided all too soon and with ease they landed on the sands.

'It was fantastic!' She couldn't stop smiling. 'I've never had any feeling like that before.'

'You'll have much more than that, and with

me.' Zeke's voice was rasping close to her ear. Swiftly he pulled her from the board, then, with another lightning movement, thrust the board ashore. Then he gripped her hand tightly and they were running full pelt up the sands and towards the secluded grove of palm trees where she had left her clothes.

He held her close and kissed her passionately, urgently possessing her mouth. The rising thrill of passion surged through her blood and she responded ardently.

He pulled her to the sands and covered her body with his. His burning arousal pressed hard against her belly and made her cling to him instintively. Quivering waves of rapture sped over her body till she felt she was melting.

She could feel his body shuddering on top of hers as she stroked his back. But with her eyes closed in ecstasy she didn't see the sudden and tormented look that changed his eyes as he focused on the beauty spot on her cheek.

To her dismay she felt a stiffening of his whole body, quite different from his sexual tension. He rolled off her quickly and lay face down in the yellow sand, labouring to regain control of his breath.

Catching her hand between his fingers, he

kissed it gently and sighed, 'Not here, Alison sweetheart. . .the timing isn't right. . .'

'I wouldn't say that. . .' she answered breathlessly, her breasts heaving.

'It's *not* right!' he rasped almost savagely. Then, as if to atone, he laid his index finger across her parted lips. 'I want it to be a beautiful experience for you. Everything must be special and perfect.'

She thought it would have been, but his look was so adamant that she remained silent.

'Damn the time!' he ground out as he looked at his watch. 'It's either interminably slow or it flashes by like quicksilver.'

He stood up shakily and turned away from her and, taking her cue from him, she reluctantly pulled on her clothes.

At last he turned back to her. 'I've got an important appointment. It can't wait. It must be settled.'

His face was drained of the zest and passion she had seen only moments earlier. Now he was grim and as if set on some distasteful purpose.

'Another time will be perfect. . .you'll see.' But his tone held doubts, and these darkly hinted inside her head that perhaps she had been foolish in some way.

He insisted on driving her back to her

apartment. And after she had waved him goodbye Alison wondered. That morning on the high seas she had lost her heart to him, and her soul, and very nearly her virginity.

CHAPTER EIGHT

WHEN Alison rode the bus to work on Monday she passed the part of the harbour where the *Neptune* lay at anchor. Perched high up on one of the masts of the tall ship sat the cat Jumper.

Such a beautiful, commanding creature, thought Alison. No wonder your master loves you! But she wasn't at all sure if Zeke loved her. What was it that had made him break off abruptly during their lovemaking? Whatever the reason, it was a fiercely powerful one, because the physical effort to stop short had been mighty.

But she had to push personal thoughts of Zeke to the back of her mind. This afternoon she was on a late shift and she would be in charge of the ward.

Mary was giving a take-over report in her office. 'Ross is great. His mind hasn't been damaged. He took one look at himself in the mirror this morning and demanded a haircut.'

Alison laughed, 'Well, that's a good start!'

'Yes, but the junior nurses who've been

carefully styling his hair in the latest fashion are most upset. He wants a short back and sides, just as the fashion was last year. Oh, there are no flies on him, except that he can't remember a few months.'

'Any new patients?' queried Alison.

'Yes, a Mrs Bassett, a dear old lady of seventy-four. She was cleaning her kitchen window and standing on the draining board when she slipped. Of course she put her arm out and her hand went straight through the glass. She's suffered severe lacerations to her hand and forearm, but fortunately no tendon or nerve injury.'

'Lucky lady,' sighed Alison.

Mary nodded. 'Zeke did the operation, and he performed a brilliant atraumatic technique, by all accounts from the OR. His gentleness in surgery will prevent a lot of unnecessary scarring and debilitation for Mrs Bassett.'

Alison's feelings of respect for Zeke as a surgeon had grown enormously every time he performed in OR. Turning her thoughts to the patient, she said, 'I suppose she has the usual compression bandage and that her arm is in elevation.'

'Yes. Watch her and see if she complains of too much pain—there's always the chance of a haematoma. But Zeke's post-operative bandages are usually excellent. He always takes special care to obliterate the potential spaces and prevent oedema.'

Having made a mental note about the new patient, Alison voiced some troubled thoughts she'd been having about Anne-Marie. 'Every time I pass that young lady she's unsettled.'

'She certainly is,' agreed Mary. 'The other day she told me she was worried about putting on weight, and then this morning I caught her munching nutty chocolate just after a full breakfast.'

'Some patients are plain peculiar at times.' Mary shook her head. 'And that reminds me, Lonnin was discharged over the weekend.'

'I'm sorry I didn't have a chance to say goodbye,' Alison said sincerely.

'No need—Lonnin asked if he could visit Ross. So I expect he'll be trundling along any time this afternoon. Incidentally, we haven't let him see Ross since he regained consciousness. Zeke thought it best for Ross to have a day or two undisturbed, but he's given the all-clear for today.'

Mary left for an afternoon's shopping, and Alison checked in on Ross.

'Hello, Miss Maynard.' His eyes were bright.

'Hello, that was clever of you, to remember my name.'

'I can remember everything before the accident, and since I woke up. I feel exactly the same in myself. Only everything has changed around me. And what's really odd is when I look in the mirror. Mrs Amos has booked me for a haircut tomorrow. I think she could have let me go down to the barber, though, but instead he's coming up here.'

'Don't rush things so. Everything in its own good time.'

'What's this shell here?' Ross placed his hand on the present that Lonnin had given him. 'Did my dad give it to me when I was out for the count?'

She picked it up and held it between both her hands. 'It's a loan from a fellow patient. Lonnin's just a young guy like you; he's lent it to you for luck. He'll be wanting it back now you're well.'

'You mean he came in here and gave it to me?'

'He visited you in the afternoons when your father was working. Although he's gone home now, I think he'll put in an appearance some time.'

'That was good of him,' the boy said wonderingly. 'I'll have to thank him.'

As Alison left Ross she saw Lonnin hovering halfway down the corridor. 'Hello,' she said. 'You're just the young man I want.'

'Hello, Miss Maynard. I hear Ross is conscious.'

'Yes, and he's very pleased about that conch you lent him.'

Lonnin's face shone with pride. 'It's always been lucky.' Then his expression became serious. 'Will you come with me and introduce us?'

'Of course.'

But Lonnin didn't follow straight away; instead he beckoned her back. 'I'm not sure what to expect. . .' He spoke hesitatingly. 'I got used to the one-way talk, but now. . . I don't know. . .it'll be like talking to a stranger and yet not a stranger.'

'I know what you mean, Lonnin,' Alison sympathised. 'The new Ross is very nice, though.'

'Not mental at all?'

'No,' she answered gently but firmly.

After some more explanation and encouragement, she led Lonnin into Ross's room. But there was no problem at all.

Ross said, 'Sit down, mate. And tell me all about this shell.'

The two lads struck up a lively conversation

from the start, and Alison chuckled to herself as she left them. Ross had woken up and Lonnin had grown up. The ward was a happier place for those two events.

Next she decided to pop in and check Mrs Bassett's hand. The old lady appeared to be dozing peacefully. A quick glance at the chart told Alison that the TPRs were all normal. Then she inspected the injured hand.

The fingertips were clearly visible, peeping out between the mass of fluffed-up gauze. The gauze extended this far to maintain firm, even pressure. Zeke had put on a neat compression bandage, and the hand was bandaged in the functional position with the fingers in mid-flexion to maintain the hand's concavity.

Alison was pleased to see that the fingertips were a good colour, and when she lightly touched them they were warm.

The old lady's eyes flickered open.

'I didn't mean to disturb you, Mrs Bassett. But we have to check, and you're doing fine.'

'I know I am, Miss Maynard.' Mrs Bassett read her name from her plate. 'Ever since I came into the hospital I've had nothing but the most splendid treatment. And especially from that young surgeon Dr Zeke.'

'He's the best,' Alison said simply. Then, 'Can you move your fingertips a little?'

'Yes, that's no problem.' Mrs Bassett wriggled them proudly.

'Keep moving them like that about twenty times at least every hour you're awake. That will prevent swelling building up in the hand. Dr Zeke has done the best possible job in the OR, but keeping the swelling down now is literally in your hands.'

'Will do,' chuckled Mrs Bassett. 'I was lucky, you know, dear—my son was in the kitchen when I fell.'

Alison listened and sat down on the bed.

'My son recently had a first-aid lecture at his works. And they told him that if you ever put your hand through glass you mustn't pull it back out again in a rush. You've got to wait until someone knocks the jagged pieces away first.'

'That's right,' Alison smiled. 'In the ideal situation where you've got someone with you who knows what to do and doesn't panic. Yes, often more damage is done when the hand is withdrawn reflexly than when it first penetrates the glass.'

Mrs Bassett's eyes shone with pride. 'Dr Zeke said my son's quick action probably saved my tendons, and if they'd been cut I'd be in plaster for three months, at least.'

'Absolutely right,' agreed Alison. 'And then

it would have taken many months more of rehabilitation. As it is, you'll probably only have the dressings on for a couple of weeks.'

She marvelled at how well the old lady accepted her injury. You could never tell with patients.

The following day Alison was again on a split shift. Not wanting to go back to her flat, she strolled into one of the many cafés near the shoreline. She had been shopping downtown, so this café was some distance from the hospital.

As she was sipping a tall cold drink she felt a pair of hands slide over her eyes.

'Bet you can't guess it's me!'

'I can't guess at all,' she laughed. She knew that voice from somewhere, but it was different somehow.

'Geoff, my knight errant from the lift shaft!' she exclaimed. 'But my goodness, how changed you look! Have you won the jackpot?' Then she remembered his gambling. 'Don't tell me you've broken the bank at Monte Carlo or Nevada or both!'

'Let's sit outside on the pavement, and I'll tell you everything. It's a bit crowded in here.'

He took her hand and guided her to an

empty table. After ordering a drink for himself, he grinned. 'I've had the most fantastic luck.'

I knew it was gambling, thought Alison, and her heart sank. 'How much have you won?' she asked laconically.

'My gambling days are over for good,' he told her. 'I've stopped riding the Black Diamond Express to Hell.'

'Whatever is that? I don't like the sound of it, so I'm glad you've stepped off.'

Geoff explained, 'It's a mythical train; it takes gamblers to Hell. But all that's in my past now.'

Alison looked into his eyes and she believed him. Gone were the sad lines, and in their place a look of pride.

'Tell me quickly, Geoff. It must be something very exciting.'

'I met Bernadette,' he said simply, but his eyes shone with love.

'Ah, a good woman. . .' Alison nodded.

'Listen, will you?' he joked. 'I met her at work, and I knew I wanted her straight away. We hit it off very well, but I couldn't bring myself to ask her out. . . Then one day I heard that she'd been off work for a while because she'd had a hysterectomy. . . It wasn't anything sinister, but she needed the operation. . .'

Now Alison began to understand. If Bernadette couldn't get pregnant then there would be no chance of Geoff's being responsible for bringing a disabled child into the world. It would be as if that threat was forever lifted from him.

'It's been a whirlwind romance,' he chuckled. 'But we know it's right for both of us. She knows everything about my family and she agrees that we should adopt children.'

'I'm so pleased for you.' Alison beamed. 'Have you taken the genetic test? I mean, now that the result doesn't matter.'

'There's no need,' he replied. 'Now, I no longer live in fear, I no longer live in hope. Now I live in freedom and in love.'

It was the most beautiful speech about love that Alison had ever heard, and what made it more marvellous was that it had come out of great personal suffering.

She was so thrilled that she left her chair and came to kiss him. 'I'm really happy for you,' she told him.

A silky softness rubbed against her bare leg, and, bending down, she looked straight into the amber eyes of the cat.

'Who's your friend?' asked Geoff, craning his neck. 'She seems to know you very well.'

'It's Jumper, Zeke's cat. She lives on the *Neptune* with him.'

'Aha!' Geoff grinned. 'I had a feeling you'd find your way on to that windjammer one day. Now tell me, Alison,' he tone was teasing, 'have you been in the captain's cabin? Have you been his first and only mate?'

She blushed and concentrated on stroking the short thick fur between Jumper's ears. She paused. 'Zeke and I have had a very stormy relationship. I thought things were better just recently, but now I'm not so sure.'

'Animals can tell more than they say. And I'm betting that Jumper here believes that you and Zeke will make a happy couple.'

'I thought you'd given up betting,' she tossed back at him. His words had struck a nerve within her.

'This isn't a bet. I think it's going to turn out to be a sure-fire thing. Zeke was always fair to me, and I'd like you two to be happy as Bernadette and myself.'

The cat licked Alison's fingers with her little rough tongue, then scampered off into the crowds, disappearing as quickly as she had come.

Alison continued with their intimate conversation. They were so engrossed that they didn't see the brown jeep pull up some yards down the street.

A tall dark man jumped out and quickly scooped up the cat. She purred contentedly against his massive chest, and as he stroked her back with his long elegant fingers his narrowed gaze rested on Alison and Geoff.

Speaking in an almost toneless whisper that had an edge of bitterness, Zeke said, 'Are you destined to be the only faithful lady in my life?'

He put the cat down on the front seat of the jeep, and she curled her paws under her chest and began to purr.

His harsh expression softened. 'And what are you doing so far away from home?' He looked knowingly at the cat. 'I'm not at all sure that I'm your only master. . .and where do you go on moonlit nights. . .?'

Jumper turned away and closed her brilliant eyes. She gave no answer but a soft rapturous purr.

Everything appeared to be running smoothly on the ward this evening. Mrs Bassett had a minor problem, but it could be solved, even if the solution was unorthodox.

The old lady had been sitting out of bed,

and now she looked a little tired as she leaned back against her pillows.

'I hate having dirty hair,' she began as she stroked the long white strands that tumbled down over her shoulder. 'When your hair's looking good it seems to perk you up generally.'

'I think we can organise a shampoo,' said Alison. 'It won't be difficult, as long as you feel you're up to it.'

'Shampoo!' cried the old lady, as if Alison had ordered the barber to come and give her a crew-cut. 'Certainly not! I haven't had soap and water on my head for the last fifty years at least!'

Alison was amazed at this revelation. 'Then what do you use? Your hair looks in perfect condition.'

'Why, brandy, of course, my dear.' Mrs Bassett indicated the bottle on top of her bedside locker. It was concealed in a thick brown paper bag.

Alison's mouth almost dropped open. This was beginning to sound curiouser and curiouser. If she hadn't known Mrs Bassett to be an extremely intelligent, well-adjusted patient she might well have wondered what was going on in her mind.

'I see you don't believe me.' The old lady

laughed. 'But my mother and my grandmother before me always swore by the stuff. I take a little cotton wool, pour a small amount of brandy on, and then rub it on to the hair and the scalp.

'I suppose it acts as a tonic,' said Alison, trying hard to follow the logic.

'Exactly, my dear. And I'm sure you've heard of men who put bay rum on their hair.'

Alison hadn't. But she was willing to accept that the brandy hairdressing treatment would work. After all, it was alcohol.

'But you're not thinking that we'll allow you to drink during your treatment, are you? That wouldn't be advisable, especially as you're taking a course of antibiotics.'

'Oh, I never let a drop touch my lips.' Mrs Bassett grimaced. 'We're a family of teetotallers. My grandfather used to love to tell the story that when he was at death's door the doctor tried to give him a little champagne disguised in an eggcup. But, as he put it, he saw through the plan, refused the alcohol and lived to tell the tale.'

Alison had to chuckle. That was a method of medicine that she'd never heard of before.

As Mrs Bassett only had the use of one hand and couldn't manage the job herself, Alison turned her skills to hairdressing. The ward was quiet but short-staffed.

Working away with the hair between her fingers, she remarked, 'It's amazing how effective this is. Your hair is shining clean and the scalp lovely and pink.' The whole procedure took very little time, and the hair dried almost immediately. Both patient and charge nurse were pleased with the result.

A junior nurse entered the room in an unexpected flurry. Anne-Marie had spilt Coke all over her bedclothes and was in tears.

'All right, I'll come and help change the bed. If you lend me a hand with Mrs Bassett I'll be with you in two shakes.'

The old patient proved to be no trouble at all. But Anne-Marie cried and apologised, causing such a fuss that Alison had to spend more time calming her than making the bed.

Because Alison had been interrupted, she had forgotten to clear away the dirty pieces of cotton wool, and they remained in a paper disposable bag by Mrs Bassett's bed. And the whole room smelt of brandy.

When Alison was finally free she made her way back to her office. She still had to write up the Kardex. Lounging in the swivel chair opposite her desk was the formidable figure of Zeke.

Immediately her heart lurched, because she remembered their exhilarating ride through the surf and their time together on the sands. 'Hello, I didn't expect to see you on the wards tonight.'

She was unprepared for the flash of anger in his dark eyes. 'I wasn't aware that I'd prescribed a saloon bar for Mrs Bassett's drug treatment. I was walking down the corridor and the smell of alcohol almost knocked me out!'

'Oh, that's nothing for you to worry about. . . I've just finished washing her hair with brandy.'

Black eyebrows knitted closely together. 'It looks as though you've had more than a tot yourself, Alison.'

'Calm down!' She laughed, trying to lower his hostile mood. 'It sounds crazy, I know, but it's abolutely true.'

'And what will your next tall story be?' He folded his arms across his chest. 'Are you about to tell me that her relatives run a bar downtown, and that they're so eager to visit they've run hotfoot straight from serving? And that her present condition is only the result of one whiff of the barman's apron? Don't try and give me any such rubbish!' he thundered. 'The woman's sozzled!'

Alison wasn't going to be intimidated by his outburst. Catching hold of his hand, she pulled him into a standing position.

'You'll just have to come and see for yourself,' she said, and, turning smartly round, she marched him into Mrs Bassett's room.

Fortunately the elderly patient had finished her doze and, opening her eyes, she greeted him. 'Ah, Dr Zeke, how pleased I am to see you! All your nurses are such a great credit to you. I've been treated like a queen, really pampered. I've even had my hair washed. I wonder you won't send someone to do a manicure or a pedicure next!'

Zeke stood looking nonplussed, while Alison nipped round and produced the used pieces of cotton wool. The smell of alcohol still clung pungently to them.

Managing a very forced smile, Zeke answered, 'Of course all my nurses here are the best.' Then, with more assurance. 'You didn't have a tot yourself, did you, Mrs Bassett?'

He's playing a remarkably tricky line this evening, thought Alison with annoyance.

'No, sir. I'm teetotal, and anyway, it's not allowed. Miss Maynard here was very firm when she explained about the antibiotics to me.'

By this time Zeke looked completely convinced. 'Hmm. . . I'll check the circulation in your fingers before I leave.'

Outside in the corridor Alison glanced up at his face. 'Now, sir,' she started, the light dancing in her eyes. She knew she'd won, and at this point he'd taken it all in good grace. 'To prove conclusively that I'm not "sozzled", shall I demonstrate by walking a straight line? I can easily follow the lines on the corridor tiles.'

He hung his head slightly, and smiled without showing his teeth. 'OK, I was wrong. I'm sorry. No one's seeing pink elephants on this ward.'

'Correction,' she laughed, 'you were seeing red.'

Zeke gazed into her eyes and they chuckled about the misunderstanding together.

Then as he thrust his hand into his white coat pocket the smile was suddenly wiped from his face. Alison watched the change incredulously. The sound of crinkling paper alerted her, and she saw the blue and red flashings of an airmail envelope.

It was as if her surgeon was immediately transported into a different world. That old remoteness glazed his eyes and he avoided direct eye-contact by looking somewhere over her shoulder.

She was afraid for him. 'What's the matter?' she asked softly. 'Is it bad news in your letter? Is someone in your family ill?'

His gaze roamed over her face, and she read only pain in his expression.

'Please let me help you, Zeke. Remember the night Ross woke up. . . I was upset because it reminded me of my fiancé. You were such a strength to me then, you've no idea. Let me help you now.'

It was as if some inner turmoil was at work inside his head. 'Everyone in my family is very well,' he replied tonelessly. 'I look after them all. Excuse me, I've a lot of work to catch up on.'

She detained him lightly with her hand in the crook of his arm. 'Don't go, please! There *is* something the matter. Why can't you tell me?'

He lifted his eyes slowly to hers. 'I'm sorry I snapped at you about Mrs Bassett—now, goodnight.'

Alison's heart was torn. There was obviously something very wrong, and she hated the fact that he would not confide in her.

Whatever the problem was, she could not believe that Zeke was at fault. He was an honourable doctor, and, to her, an honourable man.

CHAPTER NINE

TROUBLESOME thoughts of Zeke were temporarily lifted from Alison two afternoons later, when Mary revealed Anne-Marie's carefully hidden secret.

Mary was almost choking on her laughter, and her face was creased. 'Anne-Marie is pregnant!'

'What's so funny about that?' Alison couldn't see the joke.

'She got pregnant on the ward.'

Alison's eyes opened wide. 'But she's in a double hip spica!'

'Yes, I suppose with her legs wide apart the temptation was too much for her husband.'

'But. . .' Alison thought for a moment. 'She's in a room with someone else. How on earth did he. . .?'

'I don't know why we didn't tumble to it before. She always asked for a bedpan at visiting times.'

Alison remembered that she had seen the screens round the bed on the night she had first worked. 'Yes, that's right. And the old patient in with her was very deaf and used to take out her hearing aid.'

'Right,' laughed Mary. 'I never thought to ask if she was taking contraceptives or whether she should continue having them.'

'What does Zeke say?'

'I haven't heard. But he's got a sense of humour. We all have to have one to work here.' And again Mary burst out laughing.

Alison joined in. 'Of course, now it all makes sense. She complained that the plaster round her waist was too tight. But I put it down to the fact that she wasn't having any exercise, and, as she said, she was eating a lot.'

'Her husband was having exercise all right!' Mary raised her eyes to heaven.

'No wonder she looks in the pink of health,' Alison chuckled.

The afternoon progressed slowly. The patients were all eating tea when her office door was flung open. Zeke stepped into her room purposefully and closed the door. She couldn't understand why he looked furious.

'Is anything the matter?'

His eyes became black and narrow. 'Are we running a maternity unit here on my orthopaedic ward?'

'It certainly looks that way.' She grinned.

'Is that all you've got to say on the subject?' His eyes grew darker.

This is going to be a repeat of the Mrs Bassett affair, she thought gloomily.

'It did come as a shock. But you must see the funny side of it, Zeke. The whole hospital thinks it's quite a joke.'

'Have you completely lost all your faculties, woman?' he yelled. 'I had the devil of a job reducing that dislocation even when the patient was under anaesthetic. She had severe pelvic injuries and during the first seventy-two hours she might have developed paralytic ileus at any time. The bone has been slow enough to heal as it is. She should have been out of the plaster at least a month ago, and now. . .' Alison could see him clamping his jaws together very hard. 'Now she's gone and got herself in the club!'

She could see that he was in deadly earnest. But the inclusion of his phrase 'in the club' after all the medical jargon set her giggling. Knowing instantly that this was a mistake, she coughed and tried to cover her mouth with her hand.

'Dr Zeke. . .' she felt his formal title was necessary as he advanced towards her '. . .surely the situation isn't that bad?'

'The stupid woman's blowing up like a

balloon! I shall have to take her down to the plaster-room and slice off the plaster from above her belly and fit a dome. A dome. . .' he repeated, his eyes widening. 'She'll look like St Paul's Cathedral, for God's sake!'

'These things do happen,' Alison said, trying to calm him.

'Not on my ward. No, they shouldn't. And you. . .you were in charge when it happened.'

'I fail to see how I could have stopped it. Am I to check on every patient who has a bedpan at visiting time?' His attitude was beginning to irritate her now. 'After all, some long-stay wards have side-wards for conjugal rights. Even prisoners in jail are allowed——'

He did not let her finish. Suddenly he was very close to her face. 'So you think that any time you want someone sexually it's all right to just go ahead and have them?'

'No. . .' He was so close, his words so harsh and unexpected in their brutally. 'No, I didn't say that at all. I was only pointing out——'

Zeke pinned her against the desk, the weight of his body on hers making her flinch inside. 'It's all right to take who you want when you want. . .'

He held her closer and kissed her with such a bruising force that she was left gasping. 'Is this the way you'd like it, Alison?' His hot breath scorched her lips. He leaned his weight slightly off her. 'You know, I've felt like having you several times. However, I didn't rip your clothes off just because I felt like it. At times I exert self-control. . .and, when it comes to you, a great deal of control.'

'For heaven's sake,' she stuttered, trying to push him away, 'whatever comes over you at times? I'm sure it's got something to do with those airmail letters.'

'That's got nothing to do with you!' She could see the smouldering anger in his eyes.

'On the contrary, I think it has everything to do with me, and us. . .'

Zeke turned sharply and headed for the door. He was about to reach for the handle when she cried after him.

'You must talk to someone about this problem—it's eating away inside you.'

He stood stock still, let his hand fall and she heard a deep sigh. Immediately she was behind him, stroking his neck. 'Why don't you tell me now? When I see you like this it hurts me too.'

Quickly he turned and held her close, and she felt his whole body vibrating against hers. She tried to calm him further by stroking, but he jerked his head away.

'You're right, Alison, this isn't fair to you.

But the problem is so complex. . .and even now I don't know exactly how it will end. . .'

Taking her hand, he kissed her palm and spoke softly. 'One day I'll explain everything. Just trust me for now.'

And Alison knew that no more urging on her part would make him confide in her. She would have to wait until he told her. But that time of waiting, however long, would seem like an eternity.

Dawn broke early three days later, and a shaft of sunlight lit up her counterpane, making the colours glow. In the path of the beam motes of golden light hovered, making the air seem alive like the depths of the ocean.

Alison was fully awake, and she was glad that she didn't start work until after lunch.

She hadn't seen Zeke to talk to since Anne-Marie's pregnancy had been revealed. But by chance she had seen him as part of an astonishing scene, and now she thought of him not only as a liar but a dishonourable man.

Unwelcome images came vividly into her mind. And she saw again a man and a woman on a surfboard.

She had been riding home on the top deck of an open-air bus, and as she passed a secluded part of the coast where the ocean waters were blissfully calm she thought she recognised Zeke.

He was kneeling on his surfboard and using a paddle to glide on the waters. And behind him lay a young woman, resting on her back with an air cushion under her head, but her legs were bent up so that her knees hugged Zeke's sides. It was a most intimate posture, and Alison's heart contracted in pain when she saw that the beautiful young woman was very pregnant!

Desperately she wanted to be wrong, she wanted to tell herself that they were too far away for her to be sure that it was Zeke. But one thing made her sickeningly certain. It was the distinctive artwork on the surfboard. It was a portrait of Jumper, the black and white cat.

She remembered her sensually exciting time with Zeke when she had ridden the surf with him. Ha! His touching declaration of affection had been nothing but silky words. He had told her he never rode the ocean with women. He had also promised that she would be the only one to ride on his surfboard.

Zeke and his dark, hidden secrets had been an unknown quanity until now. But in the light of revelation Alison believed she now possessed all the disillusioning facts. And they hurt.

But she wouldn't let this mere male spoil her time in Hawaii. She decided to go to the Alo Moana beach and swim. It would be far too conspicuous a place for Zeke and his lover.

On the beach she slipped off her top clothes and wearing her bikini, walked languidly into the sea. The surf was calm today, not ideal for surfing. But the current was strong, and she had to swim with determined strokes to beat it.

With her head well down in the waters she practised a fast front crawl. Even though the sea was relatively calm the waves lapped up and around her head. Then she felt a sudden surge of turbulent water and something grabbed her leg.

'I didn't frighten you, did I?'

'Zeke!' She tried to conceal the rising pitch of her voice.

He stood by her side now, their bodies three-quarters submerged beneath the waves. Both his hands were around her waist, holding her firm.

'You startled me,' she said, lowering her gaze and trying to turn out of his grasp.

'Did you think I was a shark coming up out

of the depths after you?' He tightened his grip on her.

'You haven't got triple-banked teeth like a shark,' she replied. His teeth showed white and strong as he laughed. Why did he have to be so handsome? His deception caught at her heart.

His eyes were warm. 'I hear it's all happy endings at the hospital. Geoff Renton is getting married?'

Alison couldn't understand why Zeke should look so pleased about this. After all, Geoff didn't know Zeke very well.

But before she could answer Zeke tipped her chin up with his finger. 'It's time for us to have a long talk, Alison. There are things you should know. . .'

A cold chill ran over her body. She didn't want him to tell her, because she already knew.

But shouts of alarm rose over the waters, and, looking some short distance down the shore, she saw a crowd huddled over the body of a man.

'Not again!' muttered Zeke, and pulled her towards dry land. 'I think I'm going to need you. . .as a nurse. Come on!'

He sped away from her, running as if the

very devil was after him. Alison ran breathlessly to try to keep up, but she only stumbled if she trod in the deep divots he created in the sand with his powerful feet.

Zeke reached the prostrate man. Several others stood around looking like sightseers.

He yelled, 'I'm a doctor, let me through!'

The little crowd parted, and suddenly there was silence. The injured man was lying on his back, his arms and legs spread. Another man was bent over him and was pumping on his chest.

Alison was horrified. It looked as if the patient was a spinal cord injury, and the man bouncing on his chest could be doing irreparable damage.

'Stop that!' ordered Zeke. 'He's not drowned, he's conscious.'

The man looked up and backed off. 'I was only trying to help.'

'You may be well-meaning, but you don't know what you're doing,' Zeke snapped.

He examined the patient's mouth and nose to check that the airway was clear. The man was white and shaking slightly with fine tremors of shock.

'Can you move your hands and legs?' asked Zeke.

The voice was weak and rasping. 'No. . .'

'Do you feel any pain anywhere?'

Again the answer, 'No. . .'

Zeke gave Alison a grave look that she understood. The spine and spinal cord were undoubtedly damaged. Alison's blood ran cold. The man was so young; only in his early twenties, she guessed.

Breaking her train of thought, she heard Zeke ask the surrounding crowd, 'Has anyone a towel or something to cover him?'

'He can borrow mine.' A woman ran to fetch one.

'Make it two!' Zeke called after her. Then in a more subdued tone he said to Alison, 'Roll the one towel up when she brings it, and make a hard roll like a bandage. I'll need to put something under his neck to support it in extension.'

He bent over the young man. 'We'll have you in the hospital as quick as we can,' he told him.

The man didn't answer, he just swallowed and stared blindly at the sky.

'How long ago were the emergency services called?' Zeke asked the crowd.

Each one shuffled uneasily and looked from one to the other.

'You mean no one has. . .?' Zeke's voice was cold.

Alison gulped, but she knew this could and did happen, each person in the crowd thinking that someone else had done it. In reality it was better for ten people to call the emergency services than for the patient to wait on forever.

'Help me get the neck into position, then you go and phone,' Zeke told Alison.

At that moment the woman ran up with the two towels. Zeke covered the man with one and tossed the other to Alison, who quickly folded it.

Kneeling at the top of the patient's head, Zeke placed one hand under the man's chin and the other at the base of the skull. 'What's your name?' he asked quietly.

'Jarvis.'

'Right, Jarvis, I'm going to put a little traction on your neck, and the nurse here will put something under you. It'll help.'

'About this thickness,' Alison cut in. She held up the rolled towel.

Zeke eyed it. 'That's it. Slip it under when I give you the word.'

He gripped and pulled steadily and gently. 'Ease it under now, Alison.'

She pushed the towel into place.

'Good.' Zeke gave her a reassuring smile. 'Now I'll keep the traction up. Go and ring.

And ring my father too. Tell him what's happened and get him to organise the emergency theatre and Ted Hoffa. Ted Hoffa,' he repeated.

Alison didn't know any man called Hoffa, but she said the name over and over as she sped along.

'No!' she cried aloud. There was somebody using the phone. Confident in her purpose, she rushed up and took the receiver right out of the woman's hand.

'Sorry,' she gapsed. 'Accident on the beach. I've got to call. . .'

The woman was just opening her mouth and about to say something when she realised what Alison was saying. She made no protest as she saw the emergency numbers being punched.

Breathlessly Alison gave her name, the phone number and the location of the accident. 'He's a spinal injury,' she said.

'You'll need the 'copter with the drum, then,' came the calm voice over the line.

''Copter?'

'The special helicopter, ma'am. We'll see to it straight away.'

Putting down the receiver, she realised to her alarm that she had no money on her to call Zeke's father. The woman whose phone call she had interrupted was still standing waiting.

'Excuse me,' Alison said, biting her lip, 'I've got to call the hospital and arrange for an emergency theatre. I'm a nurse and I've got no money on me.'

'Oh—here, dear.' The woman pressed the coins into her hand.

'Thanks.' Alison dailled again. Mercifully old Dr Armstrong was at his desk and picked the phone up himself. She gabbled out the message.

'OK, I'll arrange all that. Lucky patient—Ted's the best spinal injuries surgeon in the US. He won't mind helping us out, even if he is visiting. Goodbye.'

After thanking the woman again, Alison ran back to the scene.

'Did you get Dad?' Zeke looked serious.

'Yes. Everything is arranged. And the emergency services are sending the helicopter with the drum.'

'Great.' Zeke reassured his patient and explained to Alison as well, 'The fanciest helicopter will take you to the hospital, Jarvis. It's especially adapted with a tube that's suspended so that when we move in the air, bank or turn, your neck will stay in the same anatomical position. This will prevent any further strain on it.'

The patient blinked, and Alison saw the fear on his face. She felt the fear in her stomach also.

'I can hear the 'copter now.' Zeke looked up, turning his head carefully and keeping the traction on the neck steady.

'Yes, there.' Alison saw a huge machine looming closer. It was shiny and brilliant like an oversized dragonfly, and its rotors beat the air with an ever-increasing angry buzz.

'He's seen us!' Zeke sounded relieved.

As the machine descended the sand whipped up and flew everywhere. Instinctively Alison covered the patient's face, for he could do nothing for himself except screw his eyes tight, and even this was an effort.

Before the 'copter had completely landed two paramedics jumped clear and ran, half crouched, half erect, towards the scene.

'Dr Zeke!' the first paramedic hailed. 'And of course, the patient is in the correct position.'

'No feeling below the shoulders. A possible C5 lesion,' Zeke answered, coming straight to the point.

The paramedic looked round. 'No need to scoop him up with the sand. There are enough people here to do a six-man lift.' Leaning over Jarvis, he said, 'We'll have you in Dr Zeke's hospital in less than two minutes.'

Jarvis blinked his eyes. He couldn't answer, because Zeke continued to maintain the traction and his mouth was therefore clamped shut.

'We'll put the collar on after the lift, when he's on the stretcher,' the paramedic decided.

Two of the men at the scene were roped in for the six-man lift. Zeke kept control of the head, Alison put her hands under the shoulders at one side, as did a bystander, the paramedics supported under the hips, and the other bystander supported the legs.

'You give the command, Dr Zeke,' the paramedic suggested.

'I'll give the order "four, six, lift," and on the world "lift" everyone is to lift in unison. Does everyone understand?'

There was a general murmur of assent.

'Four, six—lift!' Jarvis was lifted gently and laid on the stretcher.

'I'll put the collar on now,' the paramedic said. Zeke still pulled gently on the head while the thick collar was eased gently into position.

As the paramedic adjusted the collar, Zeke spoke to Alison. 'Drive my jeep back to the hospital. I'll travel in the 'copter so that we can go straight to OR.'

'OK. Where are your ignition keys?'

'In my pocket—here, on my right hip. Take the keys now.'

She unzipped the pocket of Zeke's swimming trunks and probed to find the keys. The pocket was deep, and she couldn't help feeling the hard wall of his abdominal muscles as she located the flat key. She was aware of his deeply controlled breathing.

'Are you working today?' he asked softly.

'Yes, a late shift.'

'Then as soon as I'm out of OR I'll ring you on the ward. We still have unfinished business.'

Alison knew the time in OR would be long and dangerous. Working and handling the spinal cord was fraught with danger. Any minor slip, the accidental cutting of nerve tissue, and the patient might end up in the morgue. It was the type of surgery that few surgeons liked to even attempt. You needed to be a bit of a cavalier, but a competent one. Ted Hoffa and Zeke would have to be brave, bold men with the steadiest of hands.

'Good luck.' She spoke to Jarvis first. 'And to you—I'll be waiting and praying for you.' She gave Zeke a look of tender support.

Then as soon as everyone was on the 'copter she and the rest of the bystanders were ordered back. They stood in the artificial cyclone of whirling air and flying sand and waved goodbye.

Soon the helicopter was out of sight, and the whirring sound faded. Suddenly Alison felt lost. A disturbing feeling of foreboding filled her heart. Surely nothing could go wrong? She only hoped her gut feeling would prove false.

CHAPTER TEN

YOU'RE a very trusting man, Dr Zeke Armstrong, Alison said to herself as she shuffled down the beach towards her clothes. You don't even know if I can drive, let alone handle the four-wheel-drive of a jeep.

She slipped into her T-shirt and shorts, pushed her feet into her sandals and trudged up the incline towards the road.

It was lucky that she had had some practice with four-wheel-drive vehicles. Slipping the key into the ignition, she said a silent prayer for Jarvis and the two surgeons, then headed for the hospital.

After pulling into Zeke's reserved parking space, she pocketed the keys and took them directly to his father's office. They would be safe there whatever time he came out of OR.

Although it was too early for her shift on the ward, she changed into her charge nurse's uniform and made straight for the office.

Mary Amos looked up from the roster that she was preparing. 'Goodness, you'll be working a triple shift at this rate! One at the crack of dawn, when you and Zeke rescue a drowning man, another shift now, and your own one late this evening.'

'It does seem like that. But I don't feel like being anywhere else but here at the hospital. Anyway, how do you know all about the accident? I've only just driven here myself.'

'The whole place is buzzing. You forget, it's not every day that the helicopter with the drum arrives. Or that we have the most eminent spinal injuries surgeon in our OR.'

Alison sank on to the chair. 'I've been keeping my fingers crossed ever since we saw the crowd around Jarvis on the beach.'

'Those tides and currents are lethal,' Mary continued. 'Fancy the young man not knowing that it was dangerous to dive into a wave, even if the water was only waist-deep.'

'Is that how it happened?' Alison passed her hand over her brow. Then she laughed. 'You seem to know more about the accident than I do, and I was there! Next, I'll be reading a more detailed account in the daily newspaper.'

'Don't laugh—that could be true. And a little publicity wouldn't hurt. There have been far too many exactly similar injuries at that location.'

Alison pulled a face.

'Yes,' Mary continued, 'people don't understand the power of the wave is beneath the water, and that if you dive and the current catches you it can smash you into the sand with an almighty force. It can be as forceful as if you were being hurled into reinforced concrete.'

'Jarvis is having the best treatment now, though,' Alison said slowly.

'And he had the best treatment at the time of the injury,' Mary commended. 'Don't forget that.'

This was some comfort to Alison, and she was persuaded to take an early lunch in the canteen. Mary would page her if she heard any news from Zeke.

After lunch she was eager to get back to the ward. And as she passed Anne-Marie's room she saw the young woman lying on the bed looking radiant. Her fingertips were resting lightly on top of the dome of plaster above her belly.

If I ever pass St Paul's Cathedral in London again, thought Alison, I'll never be able to do it without thinking of Anne-Marie and laughing!

She was so lost in her thoughts that she almost knocked into Lonnin Goddard. He had the biggest grin on his face that she'd ever seen.

'Sorry, Lonnin,' she apologised. 'What's made your day, then?'

He looked taller and straighter and much more the young man than when she had seen him a few days ago.

'It's my crutches and my cast brace,' he announced proudly. 'Being all scaffolded-up isn't all that bad; there are some conpensations.'

'Well, I've never heard a cast brace quite described like that, Lonnin, but go on, tell me the perks.'

'I rode the bus here, and it was full to bursting. So I was standing, and this gorgeous girl offered to give me her seat. But I didn't take it; I took something else.'

'OK, what did you take, Lonnin?' Alison could see he was mighty proud about it.

'Her phone number.' He grinned even more widely.

'Love springs eternal.' She beamed.

'Yeah, I think this spell in hospital has made me grow up, you know, Miss Maynard. It's done me a power of good. I don't think I'd have had the confidence before my accident.'

'I'm glad to hear it,' she replied. 'But mind you don't get too carried away on this date,

Lonnin. Don't let your girlfriend sit on your knee—I don't think the plaster or the knee hinges will stand it.'

He laughed outright. 'Then I'll have to sit on her knee!'

'I thought you said you'd grown up?' But she could tell that he took her teasing in good jest.

'Don't be a spoilsport,' he quipped. Then, 'I'm off to see Ross. He says he's bored, and it won't be long before he's discharged. But we're going to keep in touch.'

Alison waved him on his way. She was really very pleased with his whole progress.

She walked on and passed Mrs Bassett's room. It was empty. She had been discharged while Alison was off duty.

Back in the office, Mary hailed her. 'Look at the present Mrs Bassett sent up.'

'A box of brandy liqueur chocolates.' Alison chuckled. 'That old lady certainly had a sense of humour for a teetotaller.'

As the afternoon wore on both charge nurses became more anxious for Jarvis and for the surgeons. Mary left to go home, and at four o'clock, when they had been operating for more than seven hours, Alison could bear it no longer. She rang OR.

The charge nurse answered and sounded

very excited. 'Yes, Jarvis is in Recovery right now. The whole operation went smoothly. Ted Hoffa and Zeke removed five spicules of bone from alongside the spinal cord. Luckily they think there'll be only minimal nerve damage. The immediate paralysis was due to pressure on the cord.'

'Brilliant!' enthused Alison.

'The gods must have been smiling on Jarvis,' the charge nurse continued. 'The spicules of splintered bone were sharp. If there'd been any more rotation or torsion on the cervical spine they would have undoubtedly cut the spinal nerves. And we all know that they don't regenerate.'

Alison was filled with a rising tide of elation. 'It's the whole teamwork approach,' she said. 'If OR wasn't first-rate then all that immediate post-trauma treatment would go for nothing.'

'Thanks for the compliment. Anything else we can do for you?'

'Yes, is it possible to speak to Zeke?'

'Now that I can't do for you. As he was peeling off his surgical gloves he had a phone call. It was very odd. I've never seen him look like that—he was half thrilled, half agitated. In fact, he called his father straight away and organised him to look after his patients, and now he's run out of the hospital.'

'Gone?' Alison was stunned. That feeling of foreboding that she had felt as the helicopter flew away now returned to haunt her. 'Do you know where?'

'Sorry, it's all rather a mystery.'

After thanking the charge nurse she rang off.

And as the days passed Alison's faith in Zeke diminished. Speculation about his absence was rife. There was even one rumour that he had flown to the Himalayas. Another source swore that he had been seen at the international airport in his OR greens.

His father was particularly edgy during this time. He was keeping the truth close to his heart. All he would say, when questioned, was that he hadn't heard from Zeke but that he was sure everything would turn out well.

Alison's concern turned from frustration to anger. Zeke had promised that he would explain some mystery, he had promised he would call her directly from OR. She didn't expect an international telephone call, but a letter or a note would have been welcome.

She still hoped for the best. But she began to suspect that their relationship had no future.

* * *

'Congratulations! So you're a father at last, Zeke. But how many babies did she have?'

It had been ten days since Alison's runaway surgeon had raced from the OR. And this might have been her first encounter with him since that time. But fortunately she was concealed behind the wall in the hospital corridor.

Now she stood stock still and listened. Her heart was hammering wildly against her ribcage, and her blood was pounding so much through her veins that it was hard to catch exactly what Zeke answered. He had laughed, and she wasn't sure if he'd said three or four!

His father's voice sounded amused too. 'It doesn't surprise me that the little madam isn't pleased that you've moved her from her hiding place.'

'She'll have to do as I tell her,' answered Zeke mock-sternly.

What kind of an escapade had gone on behind Alison's back? She wasn't surprised that Zeke was a father, because she'd seen the beautiful dark-haired girl with him on his surfboard. And she'd looked heavily pregnant then.

'And babies and mother are still flourishing?' Alison heard Zeke's father again.

'Wonderfully, but I'm a bit concerned for the littlest girl. She's slightly frail.'

'Whatever you do, don't imagine you can bring them all here into the hospital, just so that you can keep a steady eye on them. We'd never live the scandal down!'

Both men laughed raucously, and Alison was disgusted. They were treating the whole matter as if it was merely a joke. And how many babies had Zeke fathered anyway? It must have been triplets or quads! No doubt he had super-stud potential.

Not wanting a confrontation, she retraced her steps and took the lift to a higher floor. She could escape through another exit that way.

But fortune had decreed otherwise. Running up a nearby stairway, she met Zeke as the lift doors opened.

'Alison! I thought I'd catch you as you came off the late shift. It's wonderful to see you.'

'Hello, Zeke, did you have a good holiday?' Her voice was flat, and, she hoped, dismissive.

He gazed at her with those steady brown eyes, that in other circumstances would have made her heart melt. 'I'm sorry I haven't been in touch. I know I promised I would, but the situation was too difficult.'

He paused, then, seeing no reaction, said gently, 'I'd like you to come back to the

Neptune with me tonight. Now. I think it would be easier if I explained everything to you there.'

'I don't think that's necessary. If you have anything to tell me, put it on a postcard.' She knew she sounded harsh, but she thought she would burst out crying.

His sigh was deep and protracted. 'All I ask is a fair hearing, Alison. Then you're free to go and make up your own mind about the whole affair.'

Reluctantly she agreed, and shortly they were speeding through the night towards the harbour.

The silence in the jeep stole up like a barrier between them. 'Tell me about the patients on 419,' Zeke invited.

'Mrs Bassett has been discharged. She left us all a big box of brandy liqueur chocolates, and Mary has kept some especially for you.'

'That old lady was a character,' he said warmly. 'I'm sure she knew that I'd bawled you out unfairly about the smell of brandy in her room, and the present was her little joke.'

'Maybe. . .' Alison avoided his glance.

'Is Lonnin still visiting Ross?'

'Yes, but he's got a new girlfriend.' Alison had to smile, in spite of her dour feelings.

'Lonnin takes her out to a different restaurant every night.'

Zeke chuckled. 'Who'd have thought that he'd turn out to be a young buck?'

And who'd have thought that my dream doctor was an old buck? she thought miserably.

She trembled as they boarded the *Neptune*. And at the top of the short flight of stairs that led down to his quarters she hesitated.

'Let me go first.' Zeke spoke softly. 'I've a surprise for you.'

Alison was wary. She must be mad, coming here like this.

He held out his hand and guided her down, and the touch of his fingers on her arm sent shivers through her. He still had the power to excite her.

On the floor in the corner of the room lay a drawer. Inside, and tightly huddled together, were the cat Jumper and several fluffy bundles.

'As you can see, Alison, Jumper has presented me with a ready made family.'

The mother cat was lying back, smiling radiantly. Her purring was clearly heard from the opposite side of the room.

'Oh, they're lovely!' Alison cried, and came

to kneel beside them. Zeke crouched beside her.

Alison stroked the mother cat's head while Zeke pointed out two black kittens, two white ones and a tiny tortoiseshell one who had been pushed to one side. He eased the stronger kittens to one side and attached the tortoiseshell baby to one of her mother's teats. Soon she began to suck strongly.

Alison's eyes misted over.

'I think the father must have been a ginger tom, judging by the colours,' Zeke mused.

'And I thought. . .' A single tear threatened to spill down Alison's cheek. She brushed it away.

'What did you think?' he asked gently.

She didn't want to look at him. 'I overheard your father talking to you in the corridor this evening. It sounded as if it was you who'd produced quads or quins.'

His face creased with laughter. 'No wonder I got a frosty reception when I first caught up with you! No, it wasn't me who was enjoying nights on the tiles.'

Alison blushed with shame. 'And it all sounded very mysterious, because I heard that your young madam wouldn't stay in her hiding place.'

He laughed outright and the cat looked at

him curiously. 'Jumper's hiding place was in this drawer on top of my underclothes. I had to move her out of my bedroom, and she took exception to that.'

Although she felt desperately relieved, this didn't last for long. The image of the young pregnant girl on the surfboard still remained unanswered.

She gazed into Zeke's tired eyes and willed that her residual misgivings were wrong. 'You'll have to paint five additions to your surfboard now.' Her pulse began to race again.

'Now, I have a confession,' he told her, and sat back on his heels.

'My sister has been having a lot of back pain in the last stages of her pregnancy. She thought it would be a good way of relieving her discomfort if she rode the gentle waves on the surfboard. So I took her out, even though I'd promised you that no other woman would be by my side on the ocean.' He hesitated. 'I didn't think you'd mind in those circumstances.'

Alison's heart leapt for joy. Why hadn't she remembered? Of course, she had helped Zeke choose the fluffy baby toy for his sister. How stupid she had been, jumping to conclusions!

'That was a wonderful idea,' she enthused, her eyes shining. 'Did it work?'

He grinned. 'Yes, but I don't know that the treatment is easily marketable.'

Then the light faded from his eyes, and he became determined. 'I think it's high time I explained the past. Come with me to the galley and I'll fix us a soft drink.'

She followed with hope in her heart. They sat at the small table and he sipped his drink before he started.

'Please hear the whole story, then you can judge me,' he said. He paused, and she nodded to him to go on. 'When I was doing my hospital training in England, I met and fell hopelessly in love with a first-year nurse. Everything was very intense and whirlwind, and we married too quickly. But my wife soon became discontented with the lot of a doctor's spouse. Soon she had affairs, and she left me many times.'

Alison bit her lip.

Traces of bitterness tinged his voice. 'But I was a fool for her and took her back every time. Then finally I thought I'd finished with her. Only she wrote to me from abroad saying she was in trouble and still loved me.' He shook his head. 'I went to look for her, but it was as if she'd vanished off the face of the earth.'

'How dreadful for you!' Alison consoled.

Zeke closed his eyes momentarily. 'I had the terrible feeling that something sinister had happened to her. So I put a private detective on the job, and he wrote to me frequently.'

'So that's why you were always in such a distressed state when the airmail letters arrived?'

'Yes,' he smiled slowly. 'The reason why I've behaved like a bastard to you, Alison, is because you have a beauty spot on your cheek exactly as my wife had. And when I first saw you in a British nurse's uniform in that half-light I could have been looking at my wife.'

She looked down at her hands. 'It's all very logical. Why didn't you explain before?'

'Male pride, I suppose. And because I didn't want to involve you in any way with the whole sordid affair.'

He took her hands in his. 'You see, I was still married, and I couldn't bring myself to involve you in an adulterous affair.'

Now she understood. His seemingly bizarre behaviour was rooted in concern for her.

He continued. 'When I rushed out of OR ten days ago I flew straight to Annapurna in the Himalayas. My wife and her lover had been crushed in an avalanche, and it had taken all that time to find the bodies. . .'

Alison squeezed his hands encouragingly. She saw him swallow hard.

'I identified her body and went to the funeral.' His eyes dulled. 'But when I walked away from the church I knew that that part of my life was forever in the past, and that now I could embark on a new one.'

He took a draught of his drink.

'Do I remind you of your wife still?' she asked, trembling.

'Not at all.' His eyes shone into hers. 'You're an excellent nurse. I knew that when you insisted that Ross had head control and you almost demanded that he have more rehab. And then, later on, when you told me about your fiancé, I knew you were a woman capable of pure and deep love. And I wanted you more than anyone in the world.'

She was thrilled to hear his declaration.

'Do you forgive me, Alison?'

'There's nothing to forgive,' she answered. 'You acted honourably for my good.' And she saw a secret smile tugging at the corners of his lips.

'Close your eyes,' he said. 'I've got a present for you.'

'Is this some game?'

'No, it's very serious. Close them.'

When he told her she could open her eyes again, he was kneeling on one knee on the floor. In his hands was a blood-red tulip.

'You look as innocent as a choirboy like that.' She looked on him with wonder. His eyes were dark and compelling.

'Take the flower; there's something inside.'

Peering into it, she saw a ring among the black stamens. It was an emerald surrounded by diamond drops. As she picked out the jewel the stamens sprang back up.

'It's so beautiful,' she sighed, brushing away some pollen that had stuck to the gold setting.

'Not as beautiful as you. I chose the tulip because of its red and black colour. Red is royal and black is sacred to the ancient Hawaiians. You will always be those two things to me.'

His words took her breath away.

As he slid on to the bench seat beside her, he whispered, 'I love you, and I always will. Say you'll take the ring and be my wife.'

'You know I love you too,' she answered, kissing his face. Something inside her made her hesitate. 'Give me a few minutes alone and then I'll give you an answer.'

'Have you doubts, then?'

She stroked his face and ran her fingertips across his upper lip. 'I just feel I have to settle something first.'

Reluctantly Zeke let her slip from his arms. 'Where are you going?' he asked.

'On deck,' Alison replied simply.

The night sky was full of big clouds and some powerful stars. A slight breeze blew through the rigging above her head. Looking up at the sky, she thought of her first fiancé, Mike. And immediately, before she could form the question in her head, it was as if she heard his reply.

'Yes, Alison. Marry Zeke; he's the right man for you now. I'm happy riding my motorbike up and down the clouds, and I know Zeke will make you truly happy.'

She blew a kiss to the heavens and saluted the stars, then ran straight back down to Zeke.

He caught her in his arms, and she snuggled against his chest. 'Yes, I'll marry you anywhere and any time you like,' she told him.

He kissed her passionately. 'How about being married on board the *Neptune* in mid-Pacific?'

'That sounds perfect. Then I really will feel like your first and only mate.'

He chuckled, then held her quietly, and

close to her ear spoke softly. 'Will you stay the night?'

'Yes.' Her answer came tremblingly, and she clung tightly to his powerful body.

'Tell me something personal, Alison. Did you sleep with your fiancé?'

Alison hestiated. 'We never did. . .'

'Ah, so you're a virgin.' His voice was like a caress. 'I shall feel very privileged to be the first.'

His words embarrassed her and she clung more tightly.

'Listen to me,' he said, smoothing her hair at the nape of her neck. 'I could have kicked myself when I lost my temper with you over Anne-Marie's pregnancy. I said that I often felt like tearing your clothes off and taking you.'

Her heart beat faster.

'Sweetheart, forgive those brutish words. It's not going to be like that between us. I love you so much, I want our lovemaking to give you the most wonderful pleasure. We're going to take our time exploring and coming to know each other's bodies.'

He held her away, tilted up her chin and kissed her eyes delicately. And any nervousness that Alison had melted away.

Zeke took her hand and led her to his bed.

As he undressed her slowly, he kissed her shoulders, her breasts, her belly and her thighs. Flames of liquid fire set her body alive with desire.

Undressing him made her excitement mount. She loved every inch of his body, his broad chest with thick tufted hair, the power in his hard muscles, and the secret sensuality of his masculinity that felt as hard as steel yet as soft as velvet. Quivers of controlled desire flickered over his muscles as he pulled her into bed.

His touch was electric. His hands and body thrilled her beyond her wildest desires. She was brought to fever-pitch, held on a plateau, then taken to incredibly higher heights of sensuality until her body ached for him and she was covered in perspiration.

Then he could hold back no longer, and as he took her innocence she thought she would melt.

The pain was short and sharp, but the thrill of their mutual pleasure was more.

After his climax Zeke lay panting by her side, and she gentled him down by stroking.

'Did I hurt you, my love?' His concern touched her heart.

'I love every inch of you,' she said, and this was all the answer he needed.

They slept entwined, Alison resting her head against his chest, and in the dawn he woke her with deep kisses.

'Shall we make love again?' he asked huskily.

Her smile was radiant. 'Aye, aye, skipper. You're my seafaring surgeon, the captain of my heart and soul and body.'

4 MEDICAL ROMANCES AND 2 FREE GIFTS

From Mills & Boon

Capture all the excitement, intrigue and emotion of the busy medical world by accepting four FREE Medical Romances, plus a FREE cuddly teddy and special mystery gift. Then if you choose, go on to enjoy 4 more exciting Medical Romances every month! Send the coupon below at once to:

MILLS & BOON READER SERVICE, FREEPOST
PO BOX 236, CROYDON, SURREY CR9 9EL.

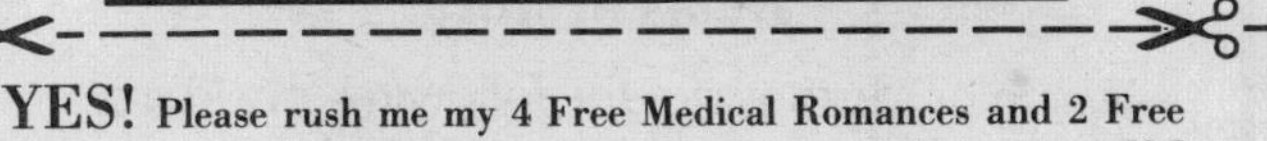

YES! Please rush me my 4 Free Medical Romances and 2 Free Gifts! Please also reserve me a Reader Service Subscription. If I decide to subscribe, I can look forward to receiving 4 Medical Romances every month for just £5.80 delivered direct to my door. Post and packing is free, and there's a free Mills & Boon Newsletter. If I choose not to subscribe I shall write to you within 10 days – I can keep the books and gifts whatever I decide. I can cancel or suspend my subscription at any time. I am over 18.

EP02D

Name (Mr/Mrs/Ms) ____________________

Address ____________________

____

____________________ Postcode ____________________

Signature ____________________

The right is reserved to refuse an application and change the terms of this offer. Offer expires **July 31st 1991**. Readers in Southern Africa write to P.O.Box 2125, Randburg, South Africa. Other Overseas and Eire, send for details. You may be mailed with other offers from Mills & Boon and other reputable companies as a result of this application. If you would prefer not to share in this opportunity, please tick box. ☐